When Darkness Comes

Book two of The World in Darkness series.

A Novel By: Michael Ross Ault

This story is a work of fiction. All incidents and dialogue, and all characters except for well know historical references, are products of the authors' imagination and are not to be construed as real. Any resemblance to persons living or dead is entirely coincidental. All product names are considered copyrighted by their owners.

Copyright 2017, Michael Ross Ault

The Story so Far

Four powerful North Korean nuclear devices, mounted on Iranian missiles launched by Venezuela from oil barges off the Gulf coast of Texas, detonate at an altitude of one hundred miles, destroying almost all complex electronics and reducing the USA to a late-1800s existence. The electrical grid from California to New York and from the Canadian border to Mexico is fried. Gas, water, sewer—and anything else requiring pumping or processing—do not work. Most people, having less than two days of food and with stores running out after less than a week, happily flock to FEMA camps with the promise of food and water. Older-model, pre-computer-controlled engines work, and some shielded electronics and military hardware still function. Cars and electronics that had been shielded in metal shelters or underground parking structures also still work.

Frank Lowman fought his way home from New York to Atlanta and then to his bug-out location in rural Alabama. Frank's wife, Katie, forced to flee their home, makes it to their BOL. After taking in Eli Anbessa, a local known to them, who had to kill the son of Reverend Sanders, a local fire-and-brimstone preacher, to keep from being lynched, Katie and friends had to face the Reverend and his fanatical followers. Frank arrived just in time to help end conflict between his family and a mob led by Reverend Sanders.

Preface to the Second Book in the World in Darkness Series

Welcome to *When Darkness Comes*. I am trying to show the effect on everyday people of a high-altitude electromagnetic pulse attack on the USA. Some people will sink to their lowest while others rise to their best. With that in mind there are two characters that seem to demonstrate this the most: William (Willie—call me Bill!) Wright Junior, and the Lowmans' friend Eli Anbessa.

But what drives these characters both evil and good ? In book one, *Prelude to Darkness*, we learned some of Eli's Eritrean background, but not much about Willie other than he is Congressman William Wright's son.

Here are two bonus chapters shining a light on both characters.

Willie

Willie Wright—he hated being called Willie but his mother had started it, so he put up with it—scrubbed diligently at his hands. It wouldn't do for one of his so-called friends to see what stained them. The remains of Sparky, the Pekingese, would never be found. Just another missing dog. That dog had barked and barked . . . barked until it was hoarse and Willie had had enough. His father said many times that the difference between a wimp and a man was that a man takes action.

Well, he'd certainly taken action against Sparky. He wondered if his dad would be proud.

Congressman Wright was very seldom proud of his only prodigy, the product of a failed, strictly political marriage with a liberal socialite. He thanked whatever deity controlled such things that she had passed from cancer. True, that had left him with Willie. The nickname suited him, the congressman thought. The boy wasn't strong enough to be called Bill or William.

Congressman Wright could not abide weakness; he sent Willie to various military boarding schools, hoping they would kick some spine into him. But with three having washed their hands of Willie, the congressman had given up and sent him to a liberal arts school. At least he'd graduated from that one and now was at New York State University at Albany, the only place that would accept him—with a generous donation, of course.

Willie was actually looking forward to this trip. He'd been selected to attend a lecture at some off-campus liberal meeting about global warming. It counted extra credit.

Personally he could care less about half the things his fellow students seemed riled up about. But liberal girls put out more than conservative ones, so anytime he could go on an overnight co-ed field trip he was game.

His walk across the quad was uneventful; it was still fairly cool, although it promised to be a scorcher later in the day. The university buildings reminded him of dominoes because the architect had lined them up in a row. The conference venue for the lecture was far enough from school that the student representatives would be spending the night. The hotel sounded nice.

At the poly sci building he met with Ms. Gert, his political science teacher, and Emily Johnson, a fellow attendee. Emily had been a minor social media star over her refusal to wear a bra at her high school; she said it sexualized women. Willie was really glad she felt that way as the cool air was definitely showing she still believed.

"Willie, I am glad you are taking an interest in Global Warming!" his professor said.

You could hear the capital letters as she said it. "It is even more important than terrorism, you know." She smiled at him.

Of course, she was ugly as a mud fence, and had been throughout the entire liberal movement, probably from the start.

"Yes, ma'am, I consider this trip vital to understanding the issues." He actually felt it was vital to get into Emily Johnson's pants.

"I wish more young men would be as concerned."

She hugged him; he tried not to tense.

"Thanks, Ms. Gert. I'll make you proud."

His smile was because he was in fact picturing doing to her what he'd done to Sparky.

Ms. Gert may have seen a shadow of it in Willie's eyes because for a moment she felt like a deer in headlights, but the feeling passed as she turned to Emily. "Watch out for him, Emily. This is his first trip."

Ms. Gert smiled at Emily, who smiled back.

"I'm sure we'll watch out for each other, Ms. Gert." Emily looked at Willie and smiled.

"I'll treat her as I would my own sister."

Willie had often fantasized about what he could do if he had a sister.

"See that you do!"

Willie volunteered to drive down to the conference in New York City. It was a short walk back across the quad to his apartment. After helping Emily load her bag into the small trunk, he opened the passenger door of his Dodge Charger for her. Usually the car's comfortable seats and overt masculinity affected even the most stalwart environmentalist chicks he chauffeured. Willie felt they secretly wanted to be dominated anyway.

"This car isn't environmentally sound, Willie," was Emily's first comment. "If I had known, we could have taken my Prius."

Willie smiled at her. "What can I say? I asked for a Prius but my dad said they were for wimps and made me get this."

He'd really wanted a Camaro, but it never hurt to empathize with chicks, especially if you took their side.

"You could always trade it in."

"My dad has it in his name."

"Your dad is Congressman Wright, isn't he?"

"Yes."

"He has the worst environmental record of all the Democrats."

"Don't remind me! Why do you think he sent me to all those boarding schools? He and I fight all the time." He neglected to mention the fights weren't about the environment.

She reached over and took his hand. Her skin was soft and warm.

"It sounds like a tough childhood."

"You don't know the half. Actually, I don't like to dwell on it. What's done is done."

"I like your attitude. Maybe if more people could let go of the past we could really do something about the problems our world is facing."

"Oh, I agree."

Like getting into her tight jeans, he thought to himself.

She let go of his hand and turned on the sound system, switching the satellite to NPR and away from his heavy metal station. By the time they reached the hotel in New York City he thought his head would explode from unicorn farts and pixie dust, as his father called the stories on NPR. It had better be worth it when he finally got her.

He parked the car as close as possible to the hotel entrance and then went around and opened her door. He helped her out and retrieved her bag from the trunk.

"After we check in let's get some lunch," he offered. "My treat."

"OK, but give me a bit to freshen up and call Carol."

"Carol?"

"My girlfriend. She is *so* possessive."

Willie was caught totally off guard. A lesbian. Maybe she was bi. He could only hope. That led him to fantasize about her and Carol, whoever she was, and him in a three-way.

"OK. Thirty minutes?"

"Sounds good. See you at the restaurant."

Willie took his bag and waited patiently with her at the elevator. She was on five and he was on sixteen, the executive level, because he'd used his father's credit card to reserve the room, an executive suite with living room, bedroom and bath. A nice fruit basket and bottled water awaited him as perks of his father's status.

After resting for twenty minutes he rose, checked his hair and returned to the restaurant to meet Emily, who was waiting right outside.

"Are you sure you don't want to go next door, Willie? This is awfully expensive."

She studied the menu posted by the door.

"Sixteen bucks for a hamburger! That's high, even for New York."

"Don't worry. Congressman Wright is picking up the bill." He flashed the titanium card; he couldn't tell if he gained or lost points, so he took it as a win.

"Don't you mean the taxpayer," she said wryly.

"Nope. This is his personal account. He said to use it for emergencies. Since it would probably be death to eat at that fast food place, I count this as an emergency."

He led into the restaurant, where they were escorted to a nice table near windows overlooking a pool in the hotel's center courtyard. Willie said wistfully, "Of course, that's how it always works."

"How what works?" Emily asked, looking over the menu.

"If I bring a suit then there is no pool; if I don't, of course there is one."

"I didn't bring one either," she said, adding teasingly, "We could always skinny dip."

"If there wasn't so much glass . . . I might be tempted."

They both knew it was impossible because all the interior rooms looked down upon the pool, not to mention the windows without blinds facing the front desk.

"Oh, well. I can always dream." Willie twitched his eyebrows, imitating Groucho Marx, and Emily laughed. For once Willie felt almost normal.

"Do you think you'll get into politics, like your dad," Emily asked, trying to make conversation.

It was cold water on Willie's mood. "No! I don't want to be anything like him. I'm not sure what I want to do."

Emily sensed the tension in Willie's voice; she was sorry she'd asked. "I hope the conference is good. They're supposed to have some compelling new data showing how much we contribute to global warming."

Willie had sat in on enough conversations between his father and his House cronies to know how much global warming was a political and not a scientific issue. He was also smart enough to know his chances of getting laid would go from nearly zero to below zero should he try to enlighten her.

"Good!" he said. "It will be refreshing to have some real facts to throw at the deniers."

After ordering, they made small talk.

Across the hotel lobby, Frank Lowman came in from an exhausting day. Unfortunately his company's salesman had oversold the product to the client, and Frank had had to enlighten them that the product really wasn't suited to their needs. Things had gone downhill from there. He was glad he was flying home in the morning.

"Look at that guy," Willie said, pointing discretely at Frank. "Schlepping that backpack full of crap all day, probably selling stuff no one wants. I can tell you that is one thing I would never want to do."

"Really? My dad is a salesmen." She looked at him coldly.

"Well, uh . . . I—"

"Oh, Willie, your face! I *am* kidding. My dad teaches school."

She laughed as Willie regained his composure.

"Well, that was mean! Just wait. When you least expect it . . ."

Willie laughed but underneath he was angry; he didn't like it when people got one over on him.

After lunch they looked at the pool and Jacuzzi, then at the exercise room, and found the lecture rooms where they would meet in the morning. Conference workers were setting up the registration table, so they both registered and collected their bags and badges.

"Let's stop by the hotel store and get some drinks and snacks for later. If you like we can get a pay-per-view in my room. After all," Willie winked at her, "Dad's paying."

"What do you think they have?" she asked, picking out some veggie chips and sparkling water.

Willie grabbed coke and chips and, at the counter, insisted on paying for everything. "My treat!" At the elevator he pressed his advantage: "Come by about seven and we'll see what's on. Room 1620."

"OK, seven-ish." She smiled at him.

At seven Emily knocked on Willie's door. He opened immediately, as if he'd been waiting for her knock. "I was afraid you wouldn't come."

He stepped back and let her into the suite.

"Wow, this is *much* nicer than the closet they gave me..."

She looked around in awe at the opulent room, taking in the multiple flat screen TVs and garden-style tub in the bath.

"My dad is platinum level, points out the wazoo. I never have to pay for a room in this chain." He couldn't help but brag a little.

"OK. So what's on?" She sat on the couch in front of the biggest TV.

"You know, if you were serious about skinny dipping, you can see the TV from the garden tub..."

"Willie, please. I like you but not that way. Like I said, I have a girlfriend," Emily said firmly, although she did give the tub another glance.

"I know, but you can't fault a guy for trying. Here's the guide; pick a movie. They include free microwave popcorn if you'd like." Willie figured it was time for plan B.

"As long as it doesn't have that artificial flavoring stuff."

"Hey, nothing but the best."

He walked to the microwave over the sink and, after tearing off its wrapper, shoved a package of popcorn into the microwave and pushed the appropriate buttons. "Did you bring your water? Or do you want something out of the honor bar?"

"In for a dime, in for a dollar. What do they have in there? I'm always afraid to open them for fear they'll charge me for the air that puffs out."

"You aren't far wrong. Let's see... gin, vodka, bourbon, scotch, red wine, white wine... several kinds of beer..."

"What the heck, I guess white goes with popcorn," she laughed, as she used the remote to turn on the TV and go to the pay-per-view menu.

Willie took the single-serving white wine bottle from the bar and, opening it, poured it into one of the suite's wine glasses. Discretely he dropped the contents of a cellophane package into the wine and swirled it into solution. Tonight would be a night to remember, at least for him.

Eli

Getting up before dawn, Eli Anbessa dressed in his cleaned and pressed UPS uniform and padded through his quiet apartment. Recently the area had been having brown- and blackouts while Alabama power replaced old transformers, so the electricity being out again this morning didn't register as unusual. Entering the small kitchen, he lit the gas stove, filled a dented aluminum coffee percolator with water, and opened a small burlap bag. Carefully he measured the darkly fragrant coffee he favored into the filter in the basket assembly. He inserted the assembly into the pot and, affixing the top, placed it on the flame. As it perked, it filled the apartment with the scent of fresh-brewed coffee.

      He was once again thankful to Allah that he had been allowed to come to the USA, where he could live free from worry about roving militia gangs and other Eritrean horrors. Once the percolator finished, Eli poured the rich coffee into a large mug, the warmth good on his strong hands. Adding three spoons of brown sugar, he drank his morning coffee with relish, just after it was cool enough not to burn.

Checking his watch, an old reliable windup Timex, Eli pushed open the screened backdoor to the modest deck and stepped into the still, cool darkness of the northern Alabama morning. It was his favorite time, that false light before dawn when the sun hadn't yet appeared. He removed his shoes and placed his prayer mat properly. After the ritual cleaning of his hands and facing Mecca as decreed by the Prophet—Allah bless and keep him—he said his morning prayers as the sun rose, bowing to Allah as he was supposed to. When he finished the last stanza of prayer and stood, he felt ready for the day. Putting on the brown shoes that matched his uniform, he pulled the UPS ball cap on his head and went out to meet his friend Abdulla. Together they would go to Martha's Café (where Abdulla was secretly in love with one of the waitresses) and have breakfast before heading to the UPS center, where they both worked as delivery drivers.

Abdulla, a Coptic Christian from Nigeria, insisted on wearing daily the traditional headdress and dark clothes. This annoyed some of the town's more ignorant people, who didn't realize he was a part of Christianity founded directly by St. Mark of the Bible.

Abdulla had use of their jointly owned car today, but he was late to pick up Eli. Odd, he was late. In the five years Eli had worked with Abdulla he had never before been late. Eli was getting worried when he saw Abdulla's readily recognizable form walking around the corner.

"My old friend!" Eli called out to Abdulla. "What has happened? Is the car broke?"

"It would not start. We shall have to rush to make the bus."

While it wouldn't take them directly to the UPS center, the DeKalb County, Alabama, rural bus service could get them within walking distance. Eli was momentarily sad that he'd miss breakfast because Martha, of Martha's café, went out of her way to provide halal certified food for him once he explained what halal was. Sometimes he envied his friend's lack of restrictions, although Abdulla was considerate, avoiding forbidden foods when Eli was with him.

Together Abdulla and Eli walked the empty streets of Fort Payne. It was peculiar they didn't see any cars. Even this early, some other folks should be going to work, too. As they rounded a corner they heard sounds of a crowd and a loud harsh voice. "My friend," Eli spoke nervously to Abdulla, "let us go around the block. Ahead is the Church of Everlasting Forgiveness."

If the church gave Eli a hard time because of his skin color and accent—and they did—what would they make of Abdulla's fierce mustache and unusual clothing, although a more gentle soul Eli had never known.

"But then we will miss the bus." Abdulla strode resolutely onward. "We can't be late."

Eli hated delivering to the Church of Everlasting Forgiveness. He didn't have a problem with Our Lady of the Valley Catholic Church, nor with any of the various Baptist, Pentecostal and other denominations. Their pastors, secretaries and other staff were friendly and greeted him pleasantly, even though he was a Muslim. Not the Everlasting folks. Reverend Sanders, when he was on the premises, was invariably gruff and acted as if touching Eli would defile him. The Reverend's son was worse, openly calling Eli names such as sand nigger, even though he was from Eritrea, miles from any desert.

As they drew nearer the church, the words of the Reverend reverberated clearly: "I tell you, brothers, it is those accursed infidels, those Muslims! They've attacked us!"

Eli and Abdulla could see the Reverend's red face. He was in full rant.

"Cowardly! They have *attacked!* And we must *defend* ourselves!"

The crowd, mostly men with nothing better to do, seemed angry as well and the murmurs Eli and Abdulla could overhear didn't bode well.

"Come," Eli said. "Let us go back before they see us."

This time Abdulla didn't argue, but it was too late.

"*There!* There are the infidels!" Reverend Sanders pointed at Eli and Abdulla. "Get them and let's get to the bottom of this!"

Several men ran toward them. Eli and Abdulla tried to flee but were soon caught and dragged back to the Reverend.

"Eli! Eli, what have you done?" The Reverend pointed at Eli. "You and your dark brothers have destroyed us."

Eli was mystified. "Reverend Sanders, I do not know what you are talking about. Abdulla and I are on our way—"

"I'm sure you were! On your way to do more *evil*. The power is out all over the country. No electronics work. It is an attack."

"Reverend, I do not know any of this. We are on our way to work."

"*Lies!*" The Reverend's eyes filled with hate. He could still see the men he'd served with in Afghanistan—or rather what was left of them after an IED blew up their patrol. Part of him remained back there.

"My friend is right. We know nothing of what you speak. Let us go!" Abdulla spoke up only to be slugged in the stomach by Malachi, the Reverend's son. Abdulla doubled over in pain.

Seeing his friend hurt spurred Eli to action. With a shoulder drop he tossed the man holding him over his shoulder as he'd been trained in the Eritrean child army many years before. Turning, he next struck the man beside him a crippling blow to the throat, and then leaped to his friend's defense. Malachi pulled a small-caliber handgun from his pocket and, placing the barrel against Abdulla's head, said, "Keep that up and he dies."

Eli felt hands grab him from behind. Then something smashed into the back of his skull, rendering the world dark.

* * *

When Eli regained consciousness he was tied securely, with Abdulla likewise secured beside him. They appeared to be in a storeroom of the church. "I am glad to see you awake, Eli," Abdulla said hoarsely.

"What happened?"

"After they knocked you out, they tied us up and put us here. They've gone off to decide what to do with us. I am afraid it will not be good."

"But why? What did we do?"

"Nothing but be different. From what I overheard, someone attacked the USA and the entire electric system is down."

Eli's eyes widened. "The entire electric system . . . there will be chaos! They are almost fully dependent on electricity."

"They blame Muslims, of course. With all the recent radical Islamic terror attacks in Europe and the USA, I cannot blame them."

"But my friend, you are Christian."

"I tried to tell them. But they laughed and said if it sounds, looks and smells like a Muslim, it is a Muslim."

"I thought I left the ignorant savages in Eritrea."

The door to the storeroom burst open and they were pulled roughly to their feet. The men hustled them into the church sanctuary. The morning light piercing stained glass windows was a strange brightness compared to the darkness of the men's faces surrounding them.

"I demand you let my friend go," Eli said bravely. "He is Christian, like you."

"Hardly, fesskin, hardly," Malachi snarled. "Look at him. Obviously a Muslim."

"Please, we were on our way to work." Eli tried reasoning again. "We mean no one harm."

"Billy Roy died. You crushed his throat."

Eli felt blood drain from his face; he hadn't meant to kill anyone. He was only helping his friend. "I am sorry. If you will get the sheriff I will go with him."

"The sheriff is busy, boy," one of the men said, holding two coils of thick hemp rope. "We know how to take care of this."

"Please, let Abdulla go," Eli pleaded once more for his friend. "He is innocent."

"You know what, I'll bet you'd like that. Let him run off to warn the others in your cell."

"We don't know what you are talking about!" Abdulla's fear was plain.

"Reverend, please. As a man of God, stop this," Eli called out as they started to drag them from the church.

"An eye for an eye, Eli. What would Mohammed do?"

Sanders smiled, but it was the smile of a carnivore.

Eli and Abdulla struggled, but Sanders' followers outmatched them. Outside a stately old oak swayed gently in the morning breeze as the man holding the ropes tossed the ends over a stout branch about ten feet off the ground.

"String up the other one first so his pal can see what he's got coming for killing Billy Roy." Malachi's smile mimicked his father's.

Forming a crude noose, they placed it around Abdulla's neck and then jerked him kicking into the air. His face purpled as the blood, trapped by the noose, caused it to swell. His frantic kicking slowed, then stilled and he hung motionless, eyes bulging. From the other side of the tree someone could be heard retching.

While everyone stared at Abdulla's slowly swinging body, Eli took a chance and stomped hard on the instep of the man holding him and then drove his head back as hard as he could, smashing it into the man's nose. Taken completely off-guard, the man collapsed, clutching his shattered nose and moaning. Turning to Malachi, Eli once again slid mentally into Eritrean combat mode and knocked him to the ground. With a few savage kicks he rendered Malachi unconscious and probably dying. Uninterested in what might happen next, Eli took off awkwardly, running with his hands tied behind him. He heard a single shot . . .

When it didn't hit him he kept running.

* * *

"Alright, what the Bejeesus Hell is going on here?"

Sheriff Wilcox lowered his service 9 mm as he stood beside Abdulla's corpse and Eli vanished around a corner.

"Sheriff, this man and the one you just let escape killed one of my followers," Reverend Sanders said, not realizing yet that his son was also probably dead.

"Sanders, in Alabama we do not take the law into our own hands." The sheriff could still see the blood lust in the men's eyes, so he held his pistol at the ready. The sheriff looked at the retching man. "Kilborn, that you?"

"Yes, Sheriff." Kilborn sounded sheepish.

"I'd thought better of you than this, Kilborn. How 'bout you tell me what happened?"

"Ah, the Reverend was tellin' us how them dirty Muslims had attacked us by cuttin' the power and all, when *they* came around the corner."

"*Who* came around the corner?"

"Eli and *that* guy." Kilborn pointed at Abdulla. Seeing the corpse made him nearly puke again.

"OK, I see. And *then?*"

"Well, the Reverend said *go get 'em*, so we could ask 'em what was going on."

"What the hell would *Eli*, whom all of you have known for years, know about any of this mess?" He gestured at the nonfunctioning power lines.

"The Reverend said they was *Muslims* and probably *sleepers*."

"He did, did he? And then . . . ?"

"Well, it got a bit confusing. Somebody slugged that fella what's now dead and Eli went berserk. He punched Billy Roy in the throat and Billy Roy choked to death." Kilborn paused, wiping puke from his chin. "After that, we all piled on and tied 'em up until we'd figure out what do."

"And . . . ?"

"An eye for an eye, Sheriff," Reverend Sanders said.

"Reverend—" a voice called out from across the yard—"Your son, he's *dead!*"

The whole group crowded around two men laying on the dew-wet grass, one holding his bloody face and moaning, the other a corpse with sightless eyes staring at the clear morning sky.

The sheriff shook his head. He had a feeling this was just the beginning.

"*Sheriff,* you must pursue that *murderer!*" Reverend Sanders screamed.

"You mean that man you kidnapped, illegally detained, and tried to *hang?* Seems to me more like self-defense." The sheriff indicated Abdulla's body. "And it also appears *you* murdered an innocent man."

"He's a terrorist! One of those *Muslims* in a secret *cell.*"

"Nope. Sorry. That man was a church-going Coptic Christian." The sheriff turned to Reverend Sanders. "Turn around and put your hands behind your back. I'm arrestin' you for the murder of Abdulla Hamarabi."

"I didn't *touch* him! Did I, men?" Reverend Sanders looked around at the crowd.

"Well?" The sheriff looked around.

"Sheriff, he didn't," Kilborn spoke up. "He never laid a finger on 'im."

"Then he incited others to commit murder."

This time, no one spoke.

"I should arrest the lot a you, but something tells me I'll be a bit busy the next few days." He looked disgusted. "I hear anything else, I *will* shoot to kill. I don't have time for this vigilante crap. Cut that man down and take him over to Wilson Mortuary."

Sheriff Wilcox closed his eyes. His face looked every one of his fifty-six years. "Two for one, seems to me justice is served. I hear of anyone going after Eli, I will take that man *out*. This is over, here and now."

* * *

Several blocks away a severe stitch in Eli's side forced him to stop running. Hobbling, his hands still tied behind his back, he sought shelter in a secluded backyard whose gate was open. The yard contained a rickety toolshed with an unlocked door that he opened with his foot. Inside it was dark but after a moment he made out rusty tools and a decrepit lawnmower. A closer study revealed a dull set of hedge cutters. He knocked the hedge cutters off the pegboard and with minimal gyrations used the blades to saw at the rope binding his hands.

It was slow work but eventually the rope parted and he was free. Rubbing his hands to restore circulation, he took stock. He couldn't go home, the Reverend and his followers could look him up in the phone directory. He had no car, because whatever knocked out the power seemed to affect vehicles as well.

Just then he heard what might be a gunshot. Peering through a wallboard gap, he watched through the open gate as a decrepit truck crept past. With another crack it backfired again, belching black smoke from the exhaust.

"It must affect only newer cars, cars with computers," Eli said softly.

He had an idea. Ms. Gilfoyle, an old lady he helped occasionally, had an ancient pickup with an equally ancient camper shell she'd once said he could borrow "anytime he needed." If he could get to her house, he might have a chance.

* * *

Back at the Church of Everlasting Forgiveness, Reverend Sanders was livid. "*Equal?* We are *far* from equal. That *infidel* killed my son!"

Deacon Carl Edwards, the only one remaining after the sheriff read the riot act and dispersed them to the local funeral home with Abdulla's body, answered, "If we do not act, we will not be respected."

"Doesn't Pete still have that old Indian motorbike?"

"I think so, why?"

"Have him patrol and watch for Eli. He's gone to ground somewhere nearby."

Deacon stood up. "OK. I'll hike over there and talk to him."

"Thanks, Deacon, you are a true friend and Christian."

"Us grunts gotta watch out for each other, Reverend." He donned his boonie cap and strode toward the sanctuary exit. "Watch your six, Reverend. He may double back."

* * *

Doubling back to the church was the last thing on Eli's mind. He was focusing all the skills he'd learned as a scout in the Eritrean child army to stay hidden as he maneuvered to Ms. Gilfoyle's house, making frequent use of backyards and overgrown shrubs. His most dangerous gambit was crossing streets. After what seemed like hours, he was knocking on her backdoor.

"Ms. Gilfoyle, this is Eli," he called out as loud as he dared. "We need to talk."

On his second hard knock, her rear door creaked open. "Ms. Gilfoyle, are you home?" Silence answered, and the house felt more than empty. The last time Eli had felt this way was when he'd searched a large hut in a village "liberated" by the child army. Everyone inside was dead.

Feeling like an intruder, Eli entered the house.

He found Ms. Gilfoyle in the living room sitting in her rocker, sightless eyes staring into the room, her hand clutching at her chest. Eli remembered her talking once about a pacemaker. With a mumbled prayer to Allah, he gently closed her eyes. She weighed next to nothing as he carried her into her bedroom and placed her in her bed. He wished he could do more; she had no living relatives. He covered her with her favorite quilt.

"Ms. Gilfoyle, I know you can't hear me but I need your truck. I know you don't care now." It felt queer, speaking to a dead body, but part of his mind was satisfied he'd done all he should. "I will send word to the sheriff about you."

Eli went into Ms. Gilfoyle's classic country pantry. He remembered her slaving over her canning—fruit preserves, canned chicken and beef, pickles. She preserved anything that grew in a garden. Most of it she gave to less-fortunate friends, or sent to distant relatives. But there was still plenty and Eli gazed lovingly at the green, gold and orange contents of the jars arrayed before him. Looked like food wouldn't be an immediate issue.

Being careful to stay unnoticed, Eli went to the old metal building that doubled as storage and garage. The squeal of the door as he slid it open made him cringe but no one seemed to pay attention. Finding wooden crates, he packed as much food as he could carry in the old truck, as well as some of Ms. Gilfoyle's deceased husband's tools. He emptied the few gallons of lawn equipment gas into the truck's tank. Eli had a moment of panic when the keys weren't in their usual place on the pegboard near the kitchen door but, luckily, he found them on the dining room table, next to a prescription she must have filled the day before.

With a prayer to Allah he returned to the garage, got in the driver's seat, pulled the choke and turned the key. After turning over a few times, the old truck's engine caught and coughed to life. It soon started running smoothly and he pushed in the choke, pleased that the engine ran so well at idle. Eli turned the truck off. He decided to overnight at Ms. Gilfoyle's and then escape Fort Payne first thing in the morning. Guiltily, he realized he'd missed afternoon prayer. It felt odd praying to Allah with a picture of Jesus holding a lamb looking down from the wall. But, according to the Quran, Jesus was one of the prophets, wasn't he? Eli was sure Allah wouldn't mind.

The next morning, Eli awoke before dawn, as was his habit. After morning prayers he wrote a simple letter explaining about Ms. Gilfoyle. A second search turned up clothes that must have belonged to her husband, which were snug on him but would fit. Eli took these, as well as a few silver and gold coins from the bottom of a desk drawer. A third search revealed no weapons other than kitchen knives; he appropriated the best. Much more ready to survive than twenty-four hours earlier, he drove away with a silent prayer of thanks to Ms. Gilfoyle and Allah for delivering him. At the sheriff's office, he dropped the note he'd written, slipping it under the door. His only concern, where to go now—

"That you, Eli?"

Shocked, Eli turned to find the sheriff standing behind him. "Yes, sir."

He held his hands out as he had seen on TV when people were arrested.

"I will go peacefully."

"Aw, shoot. Put your hands down, Eli. Fars I'm concerned, that was self-defense. I'm sorry about Abdulla. He was a good man."

"Yes, sir, he was my friend."

"Afraid those'll be in short supply in the coming times. Look, Eli, it may be smart for you to get out of Fort Payne. Reverend Sanders' son died."

Eli felt like he'd been punched. Now two more men had been added to his already large burden of guilt. "If I could take it back I would, Sheriff."

"I know. You are a good man. But I can't protect you and I don't know what Sanders will do. He ain't long on God's forgiveness."

"I was just leaving anyway. Ms. Gilfoyle has passed. I think whatever happened must have stopped her pacemaker."

"I thought that was her old truck. She'd want you to have it. Go with God, Eli."

"Inshallah, Sheriff, as Allah wills." Eli shook the sheriff's hand and Sheriff Wilcox watched as Eli climbed into the old pickup and drove off.

"Inshallah, Eli," the sheriff said under his breath as Eli motored down Jordan Road and disappeared from sight.

As Eli left the city limits, he didn't notice a man on an antique motorbike following him.

WHEN DARKNESS COMES

An Undisclosed Refuelling Base

EMP + One Week

Jimmy didn't mean to kill the president. In fact, it was the furthest thing from his mind.

Jimmy had been hungry and looking for eggs in the marsh near the base since a week ago when his daddy said something called an imp made the electricity go away. Food was harder and harder to find. The store was out of Snickers. Jimmy's parents looked worried all the time, and his dad didn't go to work anymore. Their car stopped working; everyone's did. Jimmy couldn't play games on his iPhone.

Not long ago, Jimmy wouldn't have easily gotten so near the base. But since the imp, the patrols had gotten sparse and then stopped altogether. It kind of took the fun out of it. Truth be told, the guards had enjoyed rousting and scaring the kids sneaking near the base; it broke up the monotony of guard duty.

Ahead he could hear the honks and scrabblings of the geese that colonized this part of the marsh. Jimmy liked the marsh smell—a fishy, muddy, grassy aroma. His mom was so happy yesterday when he brought home a couple eggs that he wanted to find more, so she would smile again. Carefully he watched where he placed his feet, leaving twigs unsnapped and reeds unrustled. The big birds were uncanny in their ability to sense someone near, especially now, when people were after more than eggs. He snuck up on the rookery, wary lest they chase and peck him with their long, hard beaks if he wasn't quick. In the distance he heard the startup whine of a big white plane, barely visible through marsh grass and sparse trees.

    Jimmy crept closer and closer to the birds, using the noise from the jet to hide his advances. He saw ahead the large nest of one goose and slowly, inch by inch, approached, knowing the momma goose couldn't be far distant. He reached the nest undiscovered and there were three nice eggs! The jet's noise increased and part of his mind wondered why the jet worked while his dad's car didn't. Suddenly behind him an incensed mother goose charged, squawking and honking at the egg-stealing intruder. Jimmy, trying to keep hold of the eggs and protect his tender parts, tripped on a root and plunged noisily into the silty, aromatic marsh. Jimmy's suprise aquatic intrusion startled a flock of a dozen large Canadian geese into panicked flight.

    Aboard Air Force One, President Paul was putting the last touches on a speech to the nation. A steward deferentially asked him to buckle his seatbelt for takeoff. Absentmindedly, he pushed the catch into the latch but he did not note that it failed to engage. The president felt the inertia push him into the soft seat as the huge jet hurdled down the runway and thought sorrowfully of Vice President Hayes, probably dead in the Tel Aviv dirty bomb. The rhythmic vibration of the rolling aircraft and the faint *thump-thump-thump* of tires hitting runway joints faded and transformed into smoothness as Air Force One gracefully bid earth good-bye.

The panicked geese knew one imperative: get up and away from the threat! With powerful wing thrusts they followed their flight leader up into the morning sky.

Captain Bud Hacker, pilot of Air Force One, saw the dozen large birds as they entered the starboard engines. Quite able to handle a single large bird strike, the turbines were nevertheless overwhelmed by several simultaneous strikes and began tearing themselves apart. The starboard outermost engine exploded, shrapnel tearing fuel lines and spewing high octane jet fuel before Hacker could cut off the fuel pumps. The fuel sprayed onto the hot engine, which immediately exploded in flame, destroying whatever control surfaces survived the initial engine destruction. The plane, airborne only a few hundred feet, pitched violently to the right as the wing lost lift and the portside engines drove the plane to starboard.

The president was quite unprepared for the sudden rightward pitch and, since his belt was not properly latched, became a freebody subject to the ordinary Newtonian forces of gravity and momentum, which hurled him from his seat into the bulkhead. He impacted with a dull thud and audible crack as his neck snapped. It was a merciful end, at least for the president. The rest of the crew and passengers, safely belted in, would die in the fireball.

Air Force One smashed into the marsh, pinwheeling and tearing itself apart, spewing jet fuel from its full wing tanks.

Jimmy looked on in horror as the plane impacted the birds, the right wing bursting into flame and bringing the huge, magnificent, white plane crashing to the marsh. Dropping the eggs, he ran home; maybe his dad could help . . .

Birmingham FEMA Center

Alabama

EMP + Two Weeks

Federal Judge Williams clutched the tattered black Bible in his left hand. Flanked by as much of the surviving government as could be pulled into Birmingham, Alabama, during the current crisis, he performed the hardest ceremony he had ever officiated.

On Judge William's rise to federal judge he had presided over cases where he'd had to let evil men go because of the law and watched rapists, murderers and wife-beaters go free on technicalities when he really wanted to take a bailiff's gun and shoot them dead. However, he served the law. He had to release them based on the law's precepts, knowing they would presume the law was toothless and would commit more heinous crimes.

Today was no exception.

In front of Judge Williams stood Congressman Wright. As of 09:45, when the president's plane crashed into that stinking marsh, Congressman Wright became the de facto president and now, by the laws of succession of power, he had to swear him in. The judge was privy to the backroom deals, corruption and chicanery of which Congressman Wright was part. No one came into government office as middle class and only eight years later end up a multimillionaire without dishonesty. The judge kept telling himself that the law was the law.

"William Wright, please repeat after me."

Congressman Wright put his left hand on the Bible and raised his right.

"I do solemnly swear that I will faithfully execute the Office of President of the United States, and will to the best of my ability preserve, protect and defend the Constitution of the United States."

"I, William Wright, do solemnly swear that I will faithfully execute the Office of President of the United States, and will to the best of my ability preserve, protect and defend the Constitution of the United States." Congressmen Wright smiled on the last words.

"By the power vested in me by these United States, I declare William Wright the forty-seventh President of the United States on this day, July 15, 2021."

President Wright removed his hand from the Bible and turned to the assembled government workers, military personnel and a few hundred refugees selected from the nearby FEMA camp. Looking into the few cameras present, President Wright solemnly began his acceptance speech:

"My fellow Americans, it is with great sadness I accept this position as your president. We will mourn the loss of a great man, President Paul, in a tragic accident. However, with true American spirit we must push forward with the recovery from the treacherous attack that has so paralyzed our great nation. I swear to you to work tirelessly until this nation stands once again as the shining city on the hill, a beacon of hope, power and—above all—freedom!"

He stopped for desultory applause. Most of the audience was from his district, or districts nearby, and knew that in the next election Wright would have been out on his proverbial can, and probably up on charges for various scandals.

"God, I need a drink and a hot shower," Judge Williams said to himself, leaving the ceremony. He felt dirty. He declined the invitation to the celebration.

* * *

With food shortages, no electricity and failure of water and sewage systems, the population was forced into FEMA camps across the nation. Knowing that most of Washington DC was in flames and anarchy, President Wright established a de facto capital outside the FEMA camp near Birmingham, surrounding himself with generals and men he felt he could control, if not trust.

Outside President Wright's office, Agent Smithers fidgeted with the file folder in his hands, nervous to report to the new president.

"You may go in, Agent Smithers." Cathy, the president's trusted assistant, smiled at him.

With a dry swallow, Smithers entered the president's office. President Wright sat facing a large window overlooking the now sprawling FEMA camp.

"Tell me you have good news," the president said abruptly, no friendliness in his tone; it sounded like an order.

"Eh, I am sorry, sir. We lost track of him outside of Atlanta, Georgia." He gingerly placed the file, knowing the president wouldn't like it, on the desk. "Here is everything we've found so far, Mr. President."

He stepped back.

President Wright turned and glared for a second, then snatched up the folder and silently reviewed its few pages. One picture, that of a grinning blackened corpse in the backseat of a burned-out Mercedes, slithered out and fell to the desktop. Smithers watched as the president's face colored red then darker, and the pulse in his forehead veins started throbbing.

"Garbage! All of it. Garbage." He tossed the report on top of the picture, ignoring it. "You must have followed the wrong person."

"Sir, we have DNA—"

The president held up his hand to silence him.

"You are dismissed."

Agent Smithers reached for the folder.

"Leave it. Is that the only copy?"

"Yes, sir."

"Good. I wouldn't want these lies to go any further. Get out."

Smithers hurried from the office. The president waited a few minutes then pressed the intercom for his executive assistant. "Cathy, get the acting director of the FBI."

"Yes, sir."

It took only a moment for the indicator on the president's line to light; he seized the receiver. "Acting Director Frankin for you, sir."

"Thanks, Cathy."

The line clicked over. "Director Frankin, I need to talk to you about Agent Smithers."

"Smithers? A good man, the best."

"I think he would do well to be assigned as lead agent in DC."

"In DC, sir? It is chaos there right now."

"Can you think of anywhere better for our best to be working? Get it straightened out over there so we can abandon this backwater and reoccupy our capital." The last was said with iron.

"Yes, sir. I will see to it." Director Frankin couldn't hide the capitulation in his voice.

"Good man."

President Wright hung up, not waiting for further reply. Pressing the intercom once more, he waited for Cathy. If the FBI was incompetent, maybe his pet general could handle it.

* * *

General Pratt, impeccable in his dress uniform, hurried along the industrial grey, painted corridor. He ran his hand through his military buzz-cut grey hair—a nervous habit. A dark office door window mirrored the worried expression on his careworn face, cut with wrinkles from years of field assignments in Afghanistan, Iraq and Turkey, locales with harsh winters and brutally hot summers. He'd resented being sent to Birmingham until he heard that Wright had transferred his family there, "for safekeeping," the president's letter informed him, "during this time of trouble." Pratt's highly polished black dress boots made surprisingly little sound.

The new president was not one to be kept waiting. The loss of the last president to a freak plane crash, and the vice president to likely immolation in the Tel Aviv nuclear strikes, led to the Speaker of the House as president. Speaker of the House Wright. Pratt knew Wright as well as anyone. He had no clue if Wright would be a good president; he had done passably as House Speaker. Pratt followed the scandal rumors that constantly surrounded Wright only as needed. After all, weren't all politicians more or less corrupt? If not before election, then usually within a few years of assuming office. He wished he'd paid more attention.

"General Pratt, you are ten minutes late." President Wright stated the obvious in his politician's modulated baritone.

The president was seated at an ornate black walnut desk and didn't rise to greet him or invite him to sit, so he stood. President Wright's finely manicured hands and black hair, club tan and white teeth all marked him as a professional politician.

The president drew out the silence until General Pratt felt sweat beading on his brow.

"Sit, Jim. We've known each other too long for kid's games."

The president smiled and pointed to a hard wooden chair.

"Thank you, Mr. President," the general answered in his graveled bass and sat stiffly in the upright chair.

"Jim, I'll get right to the point. As you know, Mexico, China and North Korea are going batshit while we're distracted. And did you see the latest brief from the Middle East?"

General Pratt shook his head in the negative; the brief just arrived that morning.

"It is in total chaos. We haven't heard a thing out of Israel since they nuked the capitals of Syria, Iran, Iraq and Jordan. We *know* Tel Aviv was nuked and we *think* a terrorist took out their government with a dirty bomb strapped on a damn camel! Can you believe it?" He paused and drank water; he did not offer any to the general.

"Yes, sir, I have heard the briefings."

General Pratt wondered what the hell the president was getting to.

"You have children, Jim. Two girls." The president picked up a framed photo from his desk—a pretty woman and a young boy.

"Yes, sir."

"Do they like living here on base?"

"They miss their friends but other than that, yes, they do, sir."

Pratt knew the president didn't want to hear some truths. His family actually hated the base and its restrictions, but the daily broadcasts showing the riots, dead cities, and other current American realities kept them cowed.

"Good. You know they missed picking up my son William Junior by a day. He was in New York for some stupid tree-hugger meeting."

"No, sir. I did not realize they didn't retrieve him."

"And No one else will, either." He smiled his TV smile. "We can't have it be known that the president can't keep track of his own son, now, can we?"

"No sir, I guess not."

"Good. The reason I called you in is because you run the Rangers on base."

"Yes, sir. I command the Ranger battalion stationed here."

"I want you to pick your best men; how many is up to you. I want them to find my son."

"Sir, wouldn't the FBI be better for this?"

"After that crap with Hillary and Trump? No way. Besides, I have their report right here—incompetent. I need someone I know, someone I can trust. Besides, it isn't like I have all the resources I'd have in DC before the event, is it?"

"Yes sir, correct. But my men aren't investigators, just soldiers."

"Is this too difficult an assignment? I can always ask Air Force Para-Rescue. I hear they can give your boys a run for their money."

The president took another drink of water, thereby reminding the general of his own dry mouth. "They're asking for command-level personnel over there. You have much field-level experience, Jim?"

It didn't take a genius to understand the implied threat. *Over there* was chaos, no matter the location.

"Yes, sir. Desert Storm, Desert Shield, several deployments, a couple diplomatic assignments."

"Good, good. Then this assignment should be a cakewalk."

"Yes, sir! We can handle it."

General Pratt knew veiled threats. There was a time when he would have jumped at a chance of command in an active area but, with the current conditions in the USA, now was not the time to leave family behind.

"Good. Here is the file with everything the FBI gathered, most of it drivel and conjecture."

The president pushed toward the general a manila folder with CONFIDENTIAL stamped on its cover. Pratt picked it up; there wasn't much in it. The general, slightly nauseated, perused the material and then closed the file. "Seems like the only person that might know something is this Lowman fellow."

"Get him, bring him here. I want to personally ask him why he abused my son."

The general bit his tongue to keep from saying that, according to the file, the president's son had gotten less than he deserved.

"Should I be removing this from your office, sir?" He held the file out to the president.

"Burn it if you like. I trust you won't let it fall into the wrong hands, Jim. Please tell Cathy to step in here on your way out."

General Pratt stood and saluted. Outside the door he turned to Cathy Hamm, President Wright's longtime aide. "He wants you, Cathy."

"Thanks, Jim. I hope he wasn't hard on you."

"No, I just feel like Ethan Hunt."

She looked at him curiously.

"Ethan Hunt, from *Mission: Impossible.*"

Outside Fort Payne, Alabama

William Wright Junior awakened to an itch. The Furacin soluble dressing on the chemically aggravated road rash covering his face dissolved as plasma seeped out of his damaged cells. The dripping—with an almost deliberate cream-and-plasma creep down his cheek—was a constant, maddening tickle that made him want to scratch his own skin raw.

He knew if he did, Clara would beat the tar out of him.
"You do that, it'll leave a nasty scar."
It was uncanny how she knew his thoughts.
"It itches like all hell! Damn, I hope I killed that bastard!"

Bill, as he preferred to his original nickname of Willie, kept returning to those last minutes before the capsaicin solution in the Lowman's improvised anti-personnel mines sprayed all over his road rash. The heavy mist from the compressed CO_2 cartridge discharged directly through a capsaicin solution in the mine, driving the burning chemical deep into the wounds. Before the pain nearly knocked him out and the burning solution filled his eyes, he got off one buckshot shotgun blast, grazing Frank Lowman in the elevated deer stand. Maybe Frank died from infection; one could hope.

During the pitched battle between Lowman's family and friends and Reverend Sanders' zealots, Clara managed to drag Bill, screaming, into the woods before Reverend Sanders' men got wiped out by reinforcements. She struggled to keep him still as men searched afterward for wounded and stragglers, not knowing who could be trusted. When dark finally came that hot night a week ago, she bundled Bill into one of several now ownerless cars, and drove, drove anywhere to escape.

They'd holed up in an abandoned pharmacy outside of Fort Payne, where she scrounged to find bandages and medicine to treat the worst of Bill's injuries.

"I have to take this stuff off or I'll go mad!"

She heard the desperation in his voice as she pawed though the various creams pulled out of the pharmacy wreckage, finally finding some antibacterial Triple-Ointment—good for burns, according to the label.

"Here, let me."

She carefully wiped the Furacin cream from the angry red furrows in his cheeks, bad enough when road rash alone and worse with the added aggravation of capsaicin compounding the pain and itching. She tied his hands to keep him from tearing his own flesh down to the meat and making things worse. She tenderly applied the new ointment. The cooling white cream did its work, his look of relief comical. The pain relief was almost instant.

"Wow, I wish you used this first."

Clara looked at the tube; it also contained lidocaine, a topical anesthetic. "Sorry. I'm not a nurse, you know."

She handed him a bottle of Excedrin PM. "Come on, this place is a target; we need to find someplace safer."

Bundling Bill into the old car, she drove to the nearest neighborhood. Once lower middle class, now it was mostly deserted. After the local food ran out and water and sewer service stopped, three or four days into the event, most residents took the government's offer of food and shelter at the FEMA camps near Birmingham.

Checking the front door at the first house, Clara found it unlocked, the house apparently deserted. Helping Bill in, she settled him in the main room. Drawing her .38, she checked the house for other people, finding none. Putting the gun away, she rushed back to Bill's side.

A couple of Excedrin PMs settled Bill into a fitful sleep.

Closing the door quietly, Clara examined what was left of their meager supplies. Now that Bill could sleep, she would scavenge. Grabbing her backpack, Clara hoped to find canned goods, or dehydrated goods of any kind. Bill needed food if he was to heal properly.

As she searched the neighboring houses she thought back with a cruel smile to the look on that asshole Reverend Sanders' face when she shot him. The idiot preacher had nearly gotten Bill killed. She put a stop to that.

The temperature, already stifling, seemed to climb as she went house to house. After the second house Clara's pack contained only a couple cans of soup, some stale crackers and a half jar of peanut butter. Rifling through the pantry of the third house, she heard a vehicle outside. Rushing into the living room, she opened the slats of the vertical blinds enough to see a military Humvee in the driveway next door.

The soldiers walked toward the house she'd just ransacked. "I can't believe we're on a bug hunt while the damn fesskins are taking over from Texas to California."

"When the General orders it, we do it. I'll check out this one; you check out over there."

Over there happened to be Clara's current location. She headed for the backdoor to slip out quietly but her backpack swung into a steel saucepan. She watched in horror as it slid out of easy reach across the counter and onto the tile floor with a loud crash. She froze.

PFC Talbot heard the noise. With a kick of his combat-booted foot he knocked the front door open.

"Freeze!" he yelled at the figure rushing toward the backdoor, raising his AR-4. The figure turned, revealing a stunning woman of obviously Native American lineage.

"I'm just looking for food! Please don't shoot!"

Clara put on her best doe-eyed expression and innocent look; it must have worked because the soldier lowered his rifle.

"Sorry ma'am. But we *are* looking for someone." Slinging the rifle behind his back he pulled a picture from his pocket and stepped closer to Clara, holding it out. "Have you seen this man?"

Clara stiffly took the picture. A much younger Bill smiled at her, probably from high school. She pretended to study the image, then handed it back with a shrug. "Nope, sorry."

"Listen, this guy is important. You see him, notify the local authorities."

"I'll watch for him."

As Clara turned to go, PFC Talbot gestured at her to come over.

"Look, come out to the Hummer. I'll give you some water and MREs."

Clara followed PFC Talbot out to the Hummer. "I'm staying in that first house over there," she said. "I can assure you he isn't in there."

"Good. One less house to search."

Opening the back of the vehicle, PFC Talbot pulled out a six-pack of water and a case of MREs and handed them to Clara. "You carry all that OK?"

"I'm stronger than I look."

Clara smiled. She put the water bottles into her pack and took the box from Talbot.

"Be careful, ma'am. We have a camp down near Birmingham; you'd be safe there. Have you got a vehicle?"

"Yes, sir. I will head down there tomorrow."

"Maybe I'll see you there." He smiled at her; she smiled back.

"I hope so . . . Talbot."

She read his name from his ID patch. Turning, she headed back to her and Bill's lair. She could feel PFC Talbot's eyes on her backside all the way.

Safe inside, she tore open the case of MREs and read the instructions. Soon two beef stew meals were being warmed by their flameless ration heaters. Clara unfolded a map. Once Bill felt like traveling she was certain they should get out of Alabama, and soon.

Lowman Property

North of Lake Weiss, Alabama

Several miles away from Fort Payne, Frank Lowman hesitantly removed the bandage on his face. His left arm, only grazed, throbbed; his face wound was more serious. A single 00 shotgun pellet had bisected his left cheek, leaving a gaping wound. It could have been worse; if the pellet had penetrated an inch or two further in, he'd be dead instead of so good-looking.

The wound, skillfully closed and sutured by the town doctor, was red and puffy. He hoped Willie enjoyed his capsaicin. He smiled grimly at the memory of Willie's screams. A search had turned up neither Willie nor whoever helped him escape the briars and hardscrabble surrounding the Lowman's bug-out location (BOL). They considered borrowing a neighbor's hound dog to track the fugitives but their absence was enough, or so Frank hoped.

He couldn't figure out how Willie found them. The last time he dealt with Willie, in New York City, Willie had knocked Frank unconscious and then tried to steal his car. Frank chose to exile Willie from the hotel where he and the other marooned travelers awakened to the post-EMP world, hoping never to see Willie again. He guessed that Sun Tzu was right: *Never leave a live enemy behind you.*

At nearly six-foot with a medium build, brown conservatively cut hair, hazel eyes and square-cut features, Frank was not bad-looking, before. His reflection in the bathroom mirror now reminded him of the graphic novel antihero Jonah Hex. *Well, nothing he could do about it.*

After carefully washing the wounded cheek and patting it dry, so as not to pull the stitches, he applied antibacterial cream and bandaged it up. *Next time he would shoot first.*

"Well, how's my handsome husband?" Katie, Frank's wife, stuck her head into the trailer's tiny bathroom.

"Not winning any beauty contests but passible, I guess." Turning, he carefully kissed her.

Katie, his daughter Max, their friend Eli, and neighbor Marlene and her son David had held off Reverend Sanders' men until Frank, Marlene's husband Earl and some friends reinforced them, putting the Reverend's men—the ones left—to flight. He saw concern in her eyes as he pulled back from the kiss. "What the heck. Adds to my rakish charm!"

He smiled, then winced as it pulled at the stitches.

Katie knew that under the bravado Frank suppressed his depression about the injury. She held him each night when he thrashed in the throes of nightmares, reliving the last few weeks since the EMP. She knew he experienced a lot of bad stuff before he made it back to her from New York.

"That's my tiger," she smiled at him. "And David is doing better; good thing the bullet missed the bone." David had been wounded in the fight.

"Good. We'll need all the able-bodied people we can get." He put his shirt on and came into the galley area of the trailer. "What's for dinner?"

"Believe it or not, lamb shish kebab courtesy of Eli."

"We are lucky to have him."

Eli was a Muslim immigrant from Eritrea. Before the EMP he was their local UPS delivery driver. After requesting to park his camper-backed pickup truck on their BOL, in return for helping them, he was instrumental in helping Katie and the others hold off the attackers. Before the attack he also helped train them to use their weapons.

Frank sniffed the outside air, fragrant with exotic herbs, onion, garlic and roast lamb. Earlier in the day with one of their neighbors, Eli traded fresh vegetables and labor patching a damaged barn roof for the lamb. The rest of the group was already at the makeshift plywood table, supported by sawhorses, as Katie and Frank joined them. Eli stood over a barbeque constructed of stone and scrap metal, applying a dark sauce to the cooking shish kebabs.

"Eli, if you don't get those over here soon I'll have to eat my own arm!" Earl was nearly drowning in his own saliva from the smell. Having worked hard all day weeding the gardens, he was ravenous.

Earl, stuck in London, England, after the EMP attack on America, had hitched a ride on a MAC flight. Luck brought him and Frank together at Frank's looted home. Together with George, a widower, they made it to Frank's BOL in time to defeat the Reverend's zealots.

"As soon as they are done, Mr. Earl, as soon as they are done," Eli answered, turning the skewers of meat. Having escaped from Eritrea's child army and making his way to America, Eli later fled Fort Payne when one of his friends was lynched by the Reverend's zealots.

With a flourish Eli placed the steaming skewers on a platter and carried them to the table.

After a prayer, the only sounds were appreciative murmurs of pleasure as the stack of skewers rapidly disappeared.

Outside of Fort Payne

Reverend Sanders drifted in and out of consciousness. The infected scalp wound from Clara's revolver caused alternating fever and chills. While Nick, once Willie's companion but now with the Reverend, gave lots of advice, he wasn't much practical help. After getting so many of Fort Payne's men killed—even if they were the less desirable ones—the Reverend couldn't show his face or seek help without risk of retribution. While he preached a good fire-and-brimstone sermon, he sucked at being a medic.

Sanders forced himself to take a drink of tepid water. His clothes, the same worn since the rout at the Lowman's a week earlier, hung in tatters from his emaciated frame. The fevers and chills from the infection saturated them with sweat, making his once immaculate white shirt a dirty grey and his sharp, pressed pants good only for the rag bin. The bloodstains from the head wound that had bled copiously didn't help. The drink of water didn't satisfy; his mouth still felt full of cotton.

Popping a couple of penicillin pills he found in an ancient prescription bottle in the old house's bathroom, he drank more water. So far the pills hadn't helped much. Of course, that could have been because they were over two years old.

Standing, Sanders nearly knocked over the small table near the bed. He looked in the mirror. His eyes, once aglow with the fervor of fanaticism, were bloodshot and sunken; his complexion was sallow, almost jaundiced; the wound on his scalp was swollen, its edges an angry red where they weren't black with dried blood and puss.

Using a dirty handkerchief, he pressed against the wound, wincing at the pain—a pop, more felt than heard, when the edge opened and more puss and blood saturated the already filthy cloth. Tossing it in disgust, he opened the drawer in the chest and searched until he found a clean handkerchief. Using the new cloth he forced the corruption out until there was nothing but blood. He cleaned the wound as best he could. He didn't have anything to bandage it with so he left it open to air.

Stumbling into the kitchen of the small house, his refuge since the failed attack, he grabbed the last bit of hard cheese from the nonfunctioning refrigerator and forced it down with more tepid water.

"Well, it is *good* to see you *up*, Reverend."

Nick's cheery voice startled Sanders and he almost dropped the cheese.

"You shouldn't sneak up. It could get you shot."

Reverend Sanders couldn't figure out how Nick moved so quietly. Still, Nick talked him out of the ditch where Lowman had dumped him for dead and helped him escape.

"You hungry?" He held out the remaining husk of cheese.

"No, thanks. I got something earlier." Nick smiled. He looked Middle Eastern with his olive complexion, dark hair and eyes.

Sanders couldn't remember ever seeing Nick eat. Oh, well. More for him.

"I think you need a different medicine." Nick sounded concerned.

"You're probably correct, but where to get it?"

Sanders sat on one of the wooden kitchen chairs. "I'm not sure where we are. And I'm a bit concussed, I think." Clara's bullet had knocked the Reverend nearly comatose and ironically saved his life, as he got tossed in the ditch with the dead bodies instead of captured.

"Well, not here. That's for sure. I think the car has enough gas to get us to a pharmacy." Nick sounded annoyingly cheerful.

The prospect of driving brought physical pain to Reverend Sanders. Focusing his eyes on anything further than a few feet away tortured him.

However, Nick was right. If the wound went septic he would die.

Birmingham FEMA Center

EMP + Three Weeks

General Pratt called Colonel Bromley into his office. Opening his desk drawer, he pulled a half-empty bottle of Tomatin scotch and bade him sit.

"We've been stationed together how long now, Todd?" General Pratt pulled two glasses from the same drawer as the scotch and poured two fingers worth in each.

"Five years here, sir, and two years in Afghanistan." Bromley took his glass, sniffed it, and then took a sip. "Smooth as ever."

"I have an assignment for you. Pick three good men." He sipped his scotch. "I need you to bring a man here. His name is Frank Lowman; lives over by Lake Weiss."

"Wasn't there a bit of a dustup between some fanatic minister and a local out that way?"

"Yes. The Lowmans defended themselves against a Reverend Sanders and a bunch of his followers."

"Are we acting as police now?"

"Heavens, no! Truth be told they did a service to the community."

"Then why bring Lowman here?"

"You never used to question orders."

"Is this an official order?"

"It will be, but not yet."

"Well?"

The general stood and went to the door, which he closed. Returning to his desk he placed the glass delicately then turned to Bromley. "President Wright seems to have lost his son. According to our files, which I must admit are thin, Lowman was the last to see him."

"I see."

"Bring Lowman here. And don't take no for an answer."

Colonel Bromley tossed of the rest of the scotch in one gulp and placed his glass next to the general's. "Yes, sir." He turned to go.

"Bromley..."

"Sir?"

"This is top secret. We don't need every hooligan out there looking to kidnap the president's son."

"Yes, sir."

The colonel left the executive administration building and headed over to the barracks. Some of his men had family and they spent their off-hours at base housing, a bunch of FEMA trailers hauled in last-minute, but the men he wanted were single.

"Ten shun!"

The colonel couldn't tell who called out as he entered the barracks.

"At ease. As you were," Bromley said. With his eyes he singled out Staff Sergeant Harper and signaled for him to come over. "Walk with me, Staff Sergeant." They exited the barracks.

"I need you, Mackleby and Davidson for a special assignment. Take a Hummer over to a little town just north of BFE. Gaylesville, Alabama. It should be hardball all the way. Once there, retrieve a civilian named Frank Lowman, no heat unless required. Bring him back. Make sure this isn't a Charlie Foxtrot, Sergeant."

"Whoa, Colonel, not a problem. We'll head out zero-dark thirty."

"It should be a cakewalk. I-59 has been cleared and has regular patrols."

"Yes, sir."

"Keep this quiet. It concerns the president. Here—" He handed Harper the manila folder. He knew the men needed to know the worst, if they weren't to walk into a complete CF. "Read this now. Tell the men only what they need to know."

The colonel waited until Harper skimmed the material.

"Don't kill him," Bromley said. "Don't interrogate him. Just bring him back. The president wants to talk with him personally."

Lowman Property

Near Lake Weiss

08:30 a.m.

"Base, this is Rover 1 . . ."

The voice, clearly Max's, rang loud and clear over the GFS radio link. After all, Maxine was at the hidden viewing post only a half mile away.

"Rover 1, this is Base, go ahead." Frank smiled, glad someone remembered radio discipline.

"Base, we have a Hummer with three occupants, apparently Army, approaching the drive."

"Copy that, Rover 1. Stay hidden. We will meet them."

"Roger that, Base. Rover 1 out."

"Looks like we may have some official visitors, Katie. Keep a weapon handy just in case, but don't sound the alarm unless you hear shooting."

Frank kissed Katie and grabbed an AR-15, one dropped when the Reverend's men turned and ran. He also grabbed his ball cap from the nail near the door.

Outside, Frank climbed aboard the four-wheeler and cranked it, thanking God he'd used a shipping container as a garage for his smaller vehicles. The container shielded them from the EMP. After giving it a few seconds to warm up, he toed it into gear with his left foot and applied the throttle with his right thumb.

About twenty yards from the trailer he shifted into second, and then into third, accelerating down the third-of-a-mile driveway through the trees that provided cover for the trailers and past the gardens where Eli, Earl and Marlene were weeding. He waved as he went by and noted they kept their Mosin–Nagants within easy reach. He hoped they wouldn't need the high-powered rifles today.

By the time the Hummer pulled into the drive, Frank waited, still astride the idling four-wheeler. He rested his hand casually on the .40-caliber Springfield automatic in the holster at his side. His AR-15 with the red dot sights rested in its scabbard on the side of the ATV.

The Hummer pulled up short a couple of yards down the driveway. Frank startled at the sudden, harsh loudspeaker:

"Frank Lowman? This is Staff Sergeant Harper, US Army Rangers. Can we talk?"

"Yes, I am Frank Lowman. Can I see some identification?"

A wallet flew out one window and into the dirt. The Hummer backed up so Frank could retrieve it.

The wallet contained a single item: the armed forces ID card for one US Army Ranger Staff Sergeant Harper. Frank slowly—showing his actions the entire time—picked up his radio. "Base, this is Rover 2. Have some sandwiches ready; bringing in some company."

"Rover 2, this is Base. Roger."

"Follow me," Frank called out. Kicking the ATV into gear, he accelerated around in a U-turn and back up the driveway.

"Should I follow, Staff Sergeant? Could be a trap." Sergeant Mackelby squinted, looking after Lowman's receding form.

"Look around, soldier. If they wanted to ambush us, they could have already without risking Lowman."

"Yes, Staff Sergeant. I see that now. Sorry."

He put the Hummer in gear and followed Lowman up the gravel road.

The Hummer followed Frank up to the trailer area where Frank parked the ATV and stood waiting for them.

With a show, the Rangers placed their AR-4s equipped with the SOPMOD M4 packages, one with an ELCAN Specter scope, on their backs using their single-point slings. Staff Sergeant Harper walked over to Frank and offered his hand.

"I'm Staff Sergeant Harper. These are Sergeants Mackelby and Davidson."

Frank could see Harper having a hard time avoiding staring at his wounded cheek.

"Well," Frank looked Harper straight in the eye, equal to equal, "what brings the Army to this little spot of BFE?".

The door to the trailer opened and Katie came out with a plate of sandwiches in one hand and a pitcher of tea in the other. "You gentlemen hungry? I have some nice lamb sandwiches and cold tea here . . ."

Frank indicated they should sit at the communal table. After a glance at the staff sergeant, Mackelby and Davidson joined Harper in unslinging their weapons and placing them against the table in easy reach, still not sure what to make of this self-assured couple. All three sat at the table. Katie dropped off the food, went back in the trailer and returned with three glasses full of the southern house wine—sweet tea—and paper plates.

"So, how can the Lowmans help the Army? You know a week ago we could sure have used your help."

"We heard about that little dust-up, Mr. Lowman. Actually, it's what we're here about."

"Don't tell me. You're here after the congressman's son."

Frank's comment caught them flatfooted. "Uh, yes, sir. But Congressman Wright is now the president. He was next in succession as Speaker of the House and unfortunately the president died in that plane crash a week ago, and Vice President Hayes is missing and presumed dead."

Now it was Frank's turn to be floored. "President? Holy shit! Good thing I didn't kill the little bastard."

"Ah, um, yes, it is."

Harper looked uncomfortable but he still had to do his job. "We need you to come with us, Mr. Lowman."

"Am I under arrest?"

Frank's eyes hardened and the tension level—an actual pressure—was felt by all. At the trailer door Katie waited, her finger poised above the alarm button.

"No, sir. The president would just like to talk with you about his son. It is a short ride down to Birmingham and back. A day, maybe two at most."

"I see. And if I say no?"

"We would really rather you wouldn't. Look, General Pratt will guarantee safe conduct there and back."

"The general a good man?"

Frank sipped his tea and watched Harper's eyes over his glass.

"The best, sir. You can trust him."

Frank saw no obvious tells. "I guess I better go, then." Katie went inside to start packing Frank's bag.

"Eat up," Frank said cheerfully. "We smoked that lamb ourselves and our daughter made the pickles. There might even be a bit of pear pie left over."

After they finished eating, Frank went inside the trailer to get his bag.

"Frank, do you have to go? You just got here!" Katie held back tears. Not knowing if Frank was dead or alive while he made his way home from New York after the EMP was bad enough, but now to be taken like a criminal from his own home . . .

"I have a feeling I don't have a choice. While we might get the best of the staff sergeant and his men—though I doubt it, those are Ranger emblems on their uniforms—we can't beat the entire Army."

"I know. It is just so unfair!" A single tear flowed slowly down her cheek.

Frank lovingly wiped it away. "I'll be back."

"You better, Frank Lowman. Don't let that idiot Wright railroad you."

"That's President Idiot Wright," Frank smiled grimly.

"Even worse." She hugged him tight, not wanting to let him go. "Have their doctors look at your cheek. You might as well get something out of this."

"I'll ask."

Frank kissed her. Looking out the window, he watched Harper and his men wait by the Hummer. "Well, best be moving."

Frank stepped outside the trailer and pointed to his AR-15: "Can I take my weapon?"

"If you like, sir. But we have a spare AR-4 if you'd like that instead."

Harper seemed sincere.

"It's just that I was in a convoy that got bushwhacked on my way home. Being without makes me nervous."

"We understand, sir. Here, take this one." Harper handed Frank his own weapon.

Frank released the magazine, pulled back the charging handle and checked the chamber, checked the magazine full, then slammed it home and safetied the weapon. "OK. Guess it would be presumptuous of me to call shotgun."

Harper and his men laughed. "It's safer in the back, and more comfortable."

They all turned toward the sound of the trailer door shutting.

"Here— For the ride to Birmingham . . ."

Coming down the trailer steps, Katie offered them a cooler with tea and more sandwiches.

"Thank you, Mrs. Lowman. We will take care of your husband," Davidson said, as he took the cooler from Katie and stowed it in the Humvee.

"You know, she personally killed four attackers and wounded several more." Frank smiled.

"We'll remember that." Harper smiled as well. To him, the Lowmans seemed great people. He sincerely hoped he could make good on his promises.

Frank hugged and kissed Katie one more time. "Tell Max I love her and will be back."

"I will, Frank. Be careful!"

* * *

The ride to the FEMA camp outside Birmingham was far less dramatic than the ride in from Atlanta only a week earlier. There is something to be said for regular army patrols and the application of checkpoints. Frank couldn't help but think back to when you could drive anywhere in the USA in safety, a whole three weeks ago.

Pulling into the FEMA camp, Frank watched as they passed what seemed to be miles of chain link–fenced enclosures, some with multitudes of people milling about, some still empty. The people didn't look happy. In fact, they reminded Frank of pictures from Katrina camps, and black-and-white photos of Nazi internment camps.

He thanked God he and Katie had planned ahead.

Harper parked the Hummer in front of the main administration building. "General Pratt will take you to see the president."

"Is Wright still . . ." Frank began.

"An asshole? Yes, but he is President Asshole, with emergency powers." Staff Sergeant Harper smiled. "Don't tell him I said that."

Inside the admin building, Harper took Frank down several halls and then into a somewhat sparse outer office with no admin or desk. Storage lockers lined one wall. Harper took Frank's side arm and placed it in one of the lockers. He handed the card key that activated the locker door to Frank and then indicated he should sit in the waiting room.

Keying the only item on the otherwise naked walls, an intercom, Harper said: "Frank Lowman to see General Pratt."

"Acknowledged. Please make Mr. Lowman comfortable. It will be just a few minutes."

Frank recognized the snap of command and assumed the voice that of the general. A small table and a straight-back chair where the only furnishings. On the table was a glass pitcher full of water and some glasses. Frank helped himself to the water and sat.

"Well, sir, I will leave you here. Good luck."

Harper shook Frank's hand then left the small room.

It wasn't long—enough to finish a half glass of water—before the door opened and General Pratt stepped out. "Sorry to keep you waiting, Mr. Lowman, but this is a secure storage area and I needed to copy and then put away some information." He shook Frank's hand.

"Any idea what he wants, General?"

"To talk about his son. That's all he would say. Here we are."

The general personally walked Frank into the president's compound. Cathy bade them sit in the anteroom while she announced them. She came right back out and ushered them into the president's office and closed the door.

"Mr. Lowman, so pleased you could come."

President Wright stood up from behind his desk and walked over to shake Frank's hand. The president's hand was cold, soft and clammy.

"Glad to be of help, sir." Frank thought it diplomatic not to mention he hadn't been given a choice.

"I wish all our citizens felt that way, Mr. Lowman. Tell me, are you a patriot?"

The president poured himself cold water from a pitcher on a side table. He didn't offer to Frank.

"I believe in this country, if that is what you mean."

"Yes, there is that. What about *supporting* the government?"

Frank sensed much more to the question than what was being said. "Yes, sir. As long as the government believes in the people."

The president frowned, then smiled. "I understand you know my son."

"Well—" Frank tried to sound neutral, until he got a feel for what the president was really asking—"I met him once in New York."

"I see. Wasn't it more than that?" The iron in the president's voice was cold. "In fact, didn't you attack him and basically throw him to the wolves?"

"I defended myself, sir. And did what I thought best for the other people at the hotel."

"It was best to send my son off alone?"

"Sir, *he* attacked *me*."

"You must be mistaken, Mr. Lowman."

The president made a steeple with his hands against his desk.

"I am sorry, sir. But the truth is, he brutally attacked me and tried to steal my car. And I kicked him out."

"That will be quite *enough!*" President Wright slammed his hands on the desk with a loud crash. The veins on his forehead were bulging.

"I am sorry, Mr. President. Again, I tell you it is all true."

Frank realized he was on dangerous ground.

"My son has his problems but he is *not* psychotic."

"Sir, when he didn't get his way, he attacked me and could've killed me."

"That is enough! *General!*"

General Pratt, who had been hovering outside the door, came inside.

"Arrest this man immediately for slander."

"Slander, sir?"

"He has impugned my son's character." His veins pulsed and his eyes were wild. "He is guilty of slander."

"Sir, he is within his First Amend . . ."

"The Constitution be *damned!* We are under martial law, General. The First Amendment is suspended for the duration." His lips curled into a cruel smile. "Now unless you wish to join him for insubordination to the commander-in-chief, you will arrest him."

General Pratt grew pale, then stood up straight.

For a moment, Frank thought he would stand up for what was right.

Pratt glanced at a framed picture on the president's desk. He seemed to collapse inside. "Yes, sir."

He turned to Frank. "Mr. Lowman, come with me."

Outside the office, General Pratt made Frank wait while he called some MPs. "I'm sorry, Mr. Lowman. He is the commander-in-chief and I have to follow his orders."

When the MPs arrived the general instructed them, out of Frank's hearing, and handed them a small bag.

"Sir. Please stand and put your hands behind your back," the lead MP, an imposing six-five former linebacker, ordered quietly.

"Is this really necessary?" Frank said as he stood and placed his hands behind his back.

The MP did not answer. He just put on the military handcuffs and led Frank out to a waiting Hummer.

Watching from his office window, President Wright smiled.

Outside Fort Payne

The Reverend wished Nick could drive but Nick had begged off, saying his bad leg made it nearly impossible. It sure didn't keep him from getting around. By the time they found a nearly intact pharmacy the pounding in the Reverend's head made him see double. Parking the car in the middle of the street, he slumped over the steering wheel, praying—almost for real—that the pain would stop. A trickle of puss escaped from the wound and dripped down onto the steering column. With a look of disgust he pushed up and opened the car door.

Standing made the pounding momentarily worse, and the Reverend's vision narrowed to a tunnel before the thudding of his heart quieted. His vision returned and, hobbling like an old man, he warily stepped through the broken glass door into the darkened building.

"Over here, Reverend! I think I found what you need."

Nick's voice, abnormally loud and echoing in the empty pharmacy, made the pounding in the Reverend's head worse. He stumbled toward the sound, nearly tripping on various cast-off merchandise too useless to steal. He found Nick behind the counter of the restricted area, where a pharmacist had formerly been king but was now a wasteland of broken bottles, sticky fluids and crushed pills. The Reverend noticed, with regret, that someone had already cleaned out most of the first aid shelves. He uncovered an overlooked package of butterfly wound closure strips, which he placed in his pocket along with a single roll of clean white gauze.

"What did *you* find, Nick?" Even talking drove spears of agony into his head.

Nick gestured to a shelf behind him. "I guess dopers don't steal antibiotics."

The shelf Nick pointed to was loaded with bottles, each bearing a label for a different concoction; ampicillin, penicillin, Keflex, V-cillin K, tetracycline . . . a plethora of antibiotics. Too bad the Reverend hadn't a clue which one he needed.

"Are you allergic to any of these?" Nick asked.

"Not that I know of."

Under the counter, the Reverend noticed a large red book entitled *The Physician's Desk Reference*. "Maybe this will help."

The strain of lifting the heavy book threatened him again with tunnel vision and another bout of dizziness. He climbed onto one of the tall stools by the counter until the feeling passed. Sliding the book over to a patch of light, he opened it to the section on antibiotics, where two page numbers were cited beside each drug; one led to a picture of their common forms, the other to the section about the drugs themselves. The first he searched was Ceftin, a wide-spectrum antibiotic indicated for noncomplicated skin infections, whatever the hell that meant. Leaving the book on the counter, he hobbled to the antibiotics and found a container marked CEFTIN 500 MG TABLETS. Grabbing the nearly full container, and cradling the heavy book under his arm, he stumbled back out to the car, where Nick was waiting in the passenger seat.

"I could have used your help," the Reverend said, placing the large pill bottle on the backseat floor and dropping the heavy book on the seat itself.

He opened the bottle and removed four pills, taking the bitter-tasting medicine with bottled water. Maybe he wouldn't die after all. Time would tell. He would have been surprised—and probably shot—if he and Nick had pulled up ten minutes earlier. They'd just missed Willie and Clara.

"Looks like you found what you need," Nick said. "I hear some government types are down near Birmingham."

"So . . . ," the Reverend acted confused by Nick's change of topic, ". . . what?" He took the driver's seat and started the car. The vent air, initially hot, finally turned cool and felt wonderful on his feverish skin.

"I think they will need the guidance of a Holy Man."

Was that said through a sneer? The Reverend's fever-deadened senses made it hard to be sure. "They might also have doctors. Right now I need rest."

The Reverend put the car in gear and steered slowly down the street, a wounded bear looking for a place to hole up and heal. Pulling into the first apartment without a vehicle in front, he parked the car. The effort to open his door left him trembling; he stumbled up the drive to the door.

"Hello!" He pounded on the door. "Is anyone home?"

A few blinds moved in other apartments but no one answered.

He dreaded what a kick or shoulder bump to force the door would do to his pounding head when Nick said, "Always try it, first."

Amazingly the door, unlocked, opened when he turned the knob. Inside was dark and hot. As usual, Nick was nowhere to be seen when work needed doing. Nearly passing out from the strain, the Reverend moved their meager supplies into the dark apartment. Sweat and puss streaked his face when he finished. He batted away a buzzing fly.

In the kitchen he found dishcloths and, using bottled water, cleaned under the flap of his scalp, debriding as much dead tissue from the wound gouge as he could with a paring knife. When a final rinse of the wound showed only blood, he forced the flap of scalp back down on the raw flesh and closed it with butterfly strips. He wrapped his head with gauze, tying it in place.

Pale and faint from his exertions, he retreated to a bedroom and collapsed on a bed.

Birmingham FEMA Center

EMP + Three Weeks

Sitting behind the two MPs in the open vehicle, Frank dreaded what might come next. Bad enough if it were run-of-the-mill jail but, here, he was sure it could be worse. Fenced enclosures, some empty and some with desperate-looking people, slid by the window outside. With a squeal of brakes they pulled to a stop near one of the more crowded enclosures.

One of the MPs got out. "Please exit the vehicle, Mr. Lowman."

Curious and a little afraid, Frank clambered clumsily out of the vehicle; having his hands in cuffs behind him made it difficult to balance.

"Turn around, sir."

Frank did as ordered. Would this be his execution? He could hear the MP's belt rustle as he pulled something from it. Frank closed his eyes, thinking of his family . . .

But then his hands fell loosely to his side as the MP unfastened the handcuffs.

"Mr. Lowman, we were instructed to turn you over to local authorities." The MP smiled at him. "But there *aren't* any local authorities, so we are releasing you to your own recognizance."

It took a moment for Frank to absorb this. He rubbed circulation back into his hands. "I'm free to go?"

"Yes, sir. And not that we condone theft, but there are dozens of abandoned cars over that hill there. Some probably still run. No one will mind if you 'borrow' one."

The MP handed him the small bag that General Pratt had given the MPs, saluted and climbed into the vehicle. With a slight grinding of gears, it drove off, leaving a puzzled Frank standing beside the fence.

The bag contained Frank's ID and side arm. Under them was a set of papers, which Frank unfolded and found to be travel vouchers—signed by Pratt—permitting Frank to travel to his Gaylesville home. Frank sent another prayer of thanks for the general's kindnesses but he couldn't help feeling sad, realizing that now you needed official papers to travel.

"I'll have to send the general a thank you card," Frank said to himself, heading in the direction indicated by the MP. Sure enough, over the hill was a large parking lot full of cars. Whence they came Frank wasn't sure, probably from the folks inside the fences. He vowed to return whatever transport he took. He'd wondered how to deal with any patrols that might stop him; the travel papers would handle that problem. Frank put on his holstered gun, pulled it free and checked it, then loaded it. It felt good to have it on his hip once more.

It wasn't a long walk to the first lot. It reminded him of the Park-and-Ride lot at the Atlanta airport. He soon located an old, blue, beat-up Ford Ranger with the keys over the visor. After a few turns, the engine started with a grey cloud of exhaust. The half-full gas tank was more than enough to get him home. With yet another thanks to the general and a prayer for safe travel, Frank pulled out of the lot and headed for the highway.

Outside Fort Payne

Clara hated how her face felt—all tight, her frown causing wrinkles. Forcing herself to relax, she glanced toward Bill, who, feverish and six-hours asleep, moaned softly. In the house's fireplace she started a fire to heat water for coffee. The MREs were self-heating, so she could wait until Bill woke to prepare them. She found a European-style coffeemaker in a cupboard. The blocky aluminum pot confused her until she twisted top and bottom and it unscrewed, revealing a filter between the two halves. She packed that with coffee and filled the bottom with water. She left the top open and watched it fill with dark coffee as the bottom heated and then boiled, forcing hot water through the filter unit.

"Smells good."

Bill's voice, rough and dry, startled her.

"Hi, baby. I was worried you'd sleep the day away."

She put her hand to his forehead. It felt cool and slightly damp. His fever had broken. She smiled. "I met some army guys. They gave me some water and MREs."

Following directions, she set the MRE entrées on their warmers and then set them aside to heat. She poured coffee for Bill; in spite of the heat he could use the stimulant. A cupboard door squeaked as she opened it to find sugar and dry creamer. Bill liked it blonde and sweet.

After blowing on the scalding coffee, he took a tentative sip. "Holy crap, that's good. Strong, just like I like it."

Clara was relieved; Bill seemed to be back to normal.

"Have you seen Nick?"

Clara tried to hide her quick frown—*his first non-fever-driven thought was for Nick.*

"No, not since the battle."

"I hope he wasn't hurt." Bill sipped at the coffee, his brow knitted in concern.

"He seems able to handle himself." Clara hoped Bill would let it drop. "He always lands on his feet."

"You're right. He'll catch up."

"Probably." Clara hoped never to hear Bill talk with Nick again.

When the MREs finished heating, they ate, relishing the food, and then Clara gave him the bad news: "Bill, we need to clear out. The army guys showed me your photo. They're looking for you."

Momentarily Bill looked worried. Could they have discovered the woman—or the others—he'd felt forced to kill? "Why would they want *me*?"

"Didn't say. They just warned me to 'watch out' for you."

"Too late!" He wiggled his eyebrows, trying for comedy, but it fell flat, given his facial injuries and abrasions.

"Honey, I'm serious. We need to get somewhere we can blend in."

"Well, Birmingham is out. Since last I checked, they probably came from there."

"They mentioned Birmingham. Said there were camps there where I would be safe."

"Right. My dad told me about the camps when Katrina happened. Not a place I'd want to be. He was inspecting the one near Birmingham when all this happened."

"Your dad?" Clara was intrigued; this was Bill's first mention of family.

"He is . . . *was* a congressman for Alabama."

She eyed him incredulously. "*Speaker* of the *House* Wright? *That* congressman?"

Bill nodded yes, as he sipped coffee.

"Well, hell, why don't we just go to *him*?"

"Because he *abandoned* me! He was supposed to send someone for me in New York—" Bill conveniently forgot why they couldn't find him at the hotel—"Besides, I like it out here, the way it is now."

Clara could tell by his tone that the conversation would go downhill if she pressed.

"OK. Fine. How about Atlanta?"

Bill was thoughtful. "A good possibility. Let's check it out."

The Road to Gaylesville

As Frank drove, he contemplated everything that had happened since awaking in the New York hotel to this changed world. He revisited each decision. Could he have handled the Willie issue differently? *Should* he have? What would happen if the president *didn't* find his son? Would he come after Frank and his family again?

Frank realized he was holding the old truck's steering wheel so hard his knuckles were white. He could see his pulse in the back of his eyes. He made a conscious effort to relax his clenched jaw and breathe deeply. Eventually the veins throbbing in the corners of his eyes calmed, a sign his blood pressure was retreating from redline.

He was about back to normal when he came up on his first army roadblock. Slowing, he pulled up to the Humvees making a V across the highway and the armed men guarding them. Frank rolled down the window as he approached the two sentries.

"That's good, sir. Stop right there. We need to see your ID and travel voucher."

One sentry approached the window while the other covered him.

"Here you go." Frank handed his travel papers and ID to the sentry, who studied them a few seconds.

"Sorry for the delay, sir. Have a nice day. Be watchful; there have been reports—for lack of a better term—of highwaymen. We have a patrol hunting them down, but be alert and avoid stopping for anyone." He handed Frank's papers through the window and saluted.

"I guarantee you I am heading straight back where I belong. But thanks for the warning."

Frank rolled up the window as he pulled away. The aging truck's air conditioner was already struggling with the Alabama summer heat.

The road was smooth and, other than abandoned cars pushed aside by army bulldozers, there wasn't much to see except burned-out or forlorn-looking homes and businesses. Frank wondered if the smell of wet ashes and burned wood, plastic and oil would be a permanent part of the new USA.

He was halfway home when he felt the need—a "fine one minute then screaming bladder the next" situation. Frank guessed the adrenalin surrounding the day's events had finally dissipated, and the normal alarms his body had been sending were now getting through. He caught himself looking for an open gas station and had to laugh.

Pulling to the side of the road, he got out and walked around to the passenger side. With a sign of relief he let go a powerful yellow stream. No apparent prostate problems, he concluded, given the volume and pressure. He was just shaking off when the growl of four-wheelers arose in the distance.

Clueless if the four-wheel drivers were good, bad or indifferent, Frank chose the better part of valor and got moving as fast as he could get the old truck started. It wasn't fast enough.

With a roar, three four-wheelers screeched around the corner behind him as he accelerated. His rearview and side mirrors revealed that each four-wheeler had a driver and a rider, and both appeared to be adolescent; the riders were armed with pistols and long guns. The punks yelled as they goosed the four-wheelers into their highest gears. Frank knew the huge machines were capable of eighty miles per hour on straightaways.

The old Ford Ranger started shaking at seventy, and Frank watched as the four-wheeler in the lead suddenly shot ahead. Now Frank was staring at the working end of a sawed-off double-barreled shotgun held by the lead rider. Crap, the kid couldn't be more than sixteen.

Jerking the truck to the right as the kid fired, Frank probably saved his own life. It made him mad. These weren't kids out for a joy ride; these were savages.

Gripping the wheel, Frank saw in the rearview another four-wheeler accelerating, apparently to get either beside or in front. Timing it to the millisecond, Frank jammed the steering wheel to the left, catching the four-wheeler on the middle of the rear tires.

Stable in a straight line at nearly seventy, a four-wheeler was *not* stable when the rear end was knocked sideways in what police call a pitting maneuver. As Frank sped by, the driver lost control, skewing laterally then rolling and tumbling down the asphalt. Neither rider wore a helmet; scratch two highwaymen.

Seeing that Frank wasn't going to be a helpless victim, the other two four-wheelers roared off, leaving their dead or dying companions in the road to feed the turkey buzzards and crows. They were soon lost to sight.

"Guess they didn't realize I had the superior weapon," Frank said to himself.

A few miles down the road, Frank passed what was once a rest stop. An army patrol had the two four-wheelers pulled aside and the riders face down on burning hot asphalt. Frank assumed they were dead because no living thing would willfully submit to having their face braised on a boiling hot surface.

He figured rough justice had been done and didn't bother to stop.

Lowman BOL

Frank thanked God as he pulled into the gravel drive leading to the trailers. Eli appeared as if by magic, with a Mosin–Nagant aimed directly at the unfamiliar vehicle. With a squeal of brakes Frank stopped the truck; Eli recognized him and smiled as he lowered the weapon.

"Mr. Frank! We were worried."

"So was I. Get in, I'll tell everyone what happened over dinner."

Eli laid the rifle behind the seat and climbed in.

"Base, this is Ranger 1. Papa Bear is coming in," Eli called on his radio.

Dinner—fried potatoes with onion and venison bites—filled the area between the trailers with wonderful aromas. As Frank ate, he explained what happened in Birmingham.

"Wright is nuts. He refuses to accept that his son is trouble. He had a General James Pratt arrest me for slander."

"Slander! But you said the truth." Katie was livid, the lioness protecting her mate.

"The general had the MPs release me to the local authorities." He took a drink of perry. "Unfortunately, there weren't any." He smiled. "I borrowed the truck from the refugee lot."

"How was the ride home?"

"Well, a couple of roadblocks but the general's travel voucher saw me through those easily enough. I did have to deal with some would-be robbers on the highway."

"You have to be bloody kidding," Earl chimed in.

"Nope, three four-wheelers, each with two riders. Tried to force me off the road." Frank took another drink of the peary; it was crisp, cool and smooth on the tongue.

"What did you do?" Earl asked.

"Well, the first one zoomed by and tried to shoot me with a double-barrel; I switched lanes and they missed. The second one tried to pass—I assume to maneuver the passenger into a good shooting position—so I pitted them as they tried to come by."

"*Pitted* them?"

"Yeah. Those things are unstable going any way but straight at high speed. As it went by, I simply smacked the rear wheel with the truck bumper. Sent them tumbling down the asphalt at seventy with no helmets, ass over teakettle. The survivors took off but little good it did them. The army caught them just up the road. Looked like they got summary executions."

Katy paled at his last statement. "Is it really getting that bad this soon?"

"It has been a couple weeks. You figure food ran out, water ran out, most folks aren't prepared, and so many are accustomed to instant gratification and handouts. I've said it before: the only thing preventing a sheep from becoming a wolf is opportunity and missing three squares."

"Is it over?" Katie reached over and took his hand. "I mean with President Wright?"

"I hope so. But with Wright in charge I just don't know."

Birmingham FEMA Center

"The patrols have found no sign of your son." General Pratt stood at attention before President Wright's desk. "Lowman said something to one of the men about Willie being in with that Sanders bunch."

"How the hell did he get to Alabama from Atlanta where the FBI lost track?"

"No idea, sir."

"We need to talk to Mr. Lowman again," President Wright said quietly. "Fetch him."

"Not possible, sir."

"Not possible? How so?"

"We turned him over to the local authorities."

"And . . . ?"

"They let him go."

"I am *not* pleased. *You* will fetch Mr. Lowman. And his whole miserable band. Perhaps a visit to the camp will be more persuasive."

"Sir, the camp is for those that can't, or won't, take care of themselves. The Lowmans are taking care—"

"I *don't* care. Are you disobeying my direct order?" Gone was any pretense of friendship.

"No, sir."

"Well, you have your orders."

Saluting, General Pratt turned and left the office.

* * *

On the way to the barracks to assign a squad to pick up the Lowman family, the general stopped by the communications center.

"Atten-*Shun!*" The PFC on comm duty snapped to attention as General Pratt entered.

"As you were. Private Jones, can we communicate on GPFS frequencies?"

"Not generally, sir, but it could be done."

"I need to talk with some civilians over by Lake Weiss. All they have is GPFS and a HAM setup, but they usually monitor only GPFS."

"Give me a few minutes, sir. I can patch something together."

"Do it."

"Yes, sir."

The private plugged in patch links and adjusted frequencies. In less than half an hour he turned to General Pratt: "Should be working, sir. Do you know which band they're using?"

"Not really. Can you listen in for their chatter? Should sound almost like military comms. They're maintaining pretty good comm discipline."

"Yes, sir. I'll set up a scanner and see if I can isolate their frequencies."

"Buzz me, soon as you have anything, Private. And keep this on the QT until my say so."

"Sir, yes, sir!"

General Pratt left the comm shack and sought out Lt. Colonel Bromley to pass along the president's new orders. Of course, he would also suggest they go by way of Florence, so that PFC Jones would have enough time to do his comm magic.

Lowman BOL

"Dad, you aren't going to believe this. Here . . ."

Max handed her father her GPFS radio used to monitor Eli, on point duty at the observation post.

"What, does Eli have a problem?"

"No. It's a General Pratt, wanting to speak to you."

Frank looked at the radio in his hand and then keyed the transmission button. "Frank Lowman speaking."

"Frank, this is General Jim Pratt. I've been ordered to pick you all up, and bring you to the FEMA camp. I just wanted to let you know, so you folks could pack what you need and be ready for us. We should be there in about four hours."

"Thanks for the heads-up, General. We will be ready."

"Make sure this is a CF, Lowman."

"Yes, sir, General. I guarantee it."

"General Pratt out."

Frank turned immediately to his daughter. "Max, get everyone together. We have to get to your sister's pronto."

"What did he mean, 'Make sure this is a CF'?"

"CF is military slang for *cluster fuck*. Pardon my French. He was telling us to run for the hills before they show up."

"Oh, shit! I'll get everyone moving."

Northeast Alabama, Near Fort Payne

"Whatever was in that cream is great!"

Bill was feeling much better. The medicated cream Clara had used on his wounds cleared up the irritation and nearly stopped the maddening itch. "I think it's time to head for Atlanta."

"OK, honey, whatever you say. I'll pack food and supplies; you keep resting." Clara smiled, happy to be fleeing Alabama, where there were too many army patrols for her liking.

"But first," Bill said, "we have to make a little visit." He was staring at the crumpled address—the Lowman's address—taken off one of their victims.

"What do you mean, 'little visit'? Let's just get to Atlanta." She was concerned Bill would make a mistake if he did anything but run.

"We need to visit the Lowmans." Bill smiled. "Make sure that Frank doesn't forget me."

"Oh, let's not poke the bear, darling. Let's just get out of here!"

After watching the Lowmans decimate Reverend Sanders' cutthroats—and nearly getting Bill killed, too—Clara wanted nothing to do with them ever again.

"I have to, Clara. I owe Frank for New York, and for this last week of misery."

"But Bill, I'm sure he hasn't been happy either." Clara hated the way she sounded. "You *did* shoot him full of buckshot."

"Clara, are you getting soft on me?"

"No."

"OK, then. It's settled. We swing by and leave Frank a good-bye he won't forget."

Bill pulled out a paper map and began plotting a route to Atlanta that would avoid major towns and roads. They couldn't afford to get stopped by an army roadblock.

* * *

Back at the Lowmans, Max finished packing her bug-out bag and stowing her spare equipment in the lockup. Frank stuck his head in the door.

"Max, could you go down and spell Eli on lookout, so he can pack?"

"Sure thing, Dad. Toss this stuff in the truck for me, will you?"

She gave him the smile that had twisted him around her finger since she'd been able to smile. "You got it, little-bit!"

It embarrassed her when he used his favorite nickname, but it also made her feel warm and loved inside. "Take the four-wheeler. We need to get out of here quick."

"Sure thing, Dad."

She slung her AR-15 over her shoulder. She'd swapped the heavy Mosin–Nagant for an AR-15 captured from Reverend Sanders' men. The AR-15 was lighter and shorter, which made it easier to use in the woods near the observation post. She climbed aboard the quad-runner and took off down the trail to the post. She would miss the BOL, its pond and gardens.

Stopping the quad near the OP, she called out, "Eli, this is Max. I am coming in."

Eli met her at the OP door. "Sure thing, Miss Max. What's wrong? I have two more hours of duty."

Max explained about bugging out. With a frown, Eli climbed aboard the quad and headed back to the main camp, leaving Max at the OP.

Placing the sound-amplifying headset on her head, Max settled down to cover the last couple hours before they bugged out. A loadout vest with survival gear and spare ammo for the AR-15 still couldn't hide her blond beauty. Her gear included spare batteries for the amplifying headphones but, unfortunately, she didn't check their battery status and left nearly depleted ones in place.

* * *

Bill and Clara parked their car about a half-mile short of the Lowman property. Clara chose to stay with the vehicle while Bill snuck over to take a look. As he neared the property he could see the top of the OP. Being as stealthy as he could, he crept up on the location.

Normally, Max would have heard him coming but the weakened batteries in the headset allowed him to get right behind her before she realized her position was compromised. With a vicious swipe, he pistol-whipped her, knocking the headset to the ground and Max unconscious.

Bill gleefully tossed Max's unconscious body over his shoulder and, holding her AR-15 in his right hand, hiked back to Clara and their waiting vehicle.

* * *

It was nearing the four-hour point when Katie tried to reach Max at the OP. "Observation Post 1, come in . . ." It was Katie's third attempt to reach Max. "Frank, come in . . ."

"Frank, here. What's wrong, Katie?"

"I can't reach Max. Could you swing by and collect her? It's time to go."

"10-4. I'll swing by and collect her. Frank, out."

Frank finished a last run through the garden, collecting fresh produce before they bugged out. The quad-runner's front and rear baskets were loaded with tomatoes, peppers, cucumbers and other produce. As he neared the OP he parked the quad and turned it off.

"Hello, the post! This is Frank . . ." he called out, but received no answering hail from Max.

Climbing off the now silent quad, he carefully approached the OP, making sure he wouldn't startle Max. He didn't want to get shot by his own daughter. All he found was the bloodstained amplifying headphones and a trail of footprints leading away from the property.

"Katie!" Frank shouted into the GPFS radio. "Looks like someone has grabbed Max."

"Are you sure?"

"Yes. I'm going to try and follow. Finish getting everyone set to go."

"Will do. Find my baby, Frank!"

"Roger." Clipping the radio to his belt, he knelt and examined the ground around the observation post. At the edge nearest the property boundary, he spotted a track from a sports shoe.

With a sickening feeling, he remembered that tread. It was the same tread from the tracks found beneath the deer stand after the battle with the Reverend's zealots—the track of Willie Wright's high-end sports shoes. Because everyone at the BOL wore hiking boots, he knew this must be from whoever grabbed Max. The tracks led to the edge of the property near the road. Frank checked up and down the roadside on both sides, hoping that the tracks would resume, but without luck. Grabbing his radio he pushed the talk button angrily, nearly breaking it.

"Katie, looks like someone has taken her by car. I lost the damn trail." He didn't want her to freak out, so he didn't mention his suspicion it was Willie.

Katie heard the anger and fear in Frank's voice. "Roger. Come back up here and get a vehicle."

"Roger."

Frank hurried back, jumping on the quad and kicking it into top gear, tearing up the half-mile trail to the main camp. "I want all of you to head to Martha's. I will try to follow whoever took Max, and get her back." Frank gritted his teeth, fighting back his fear for Max's life.

"Oh, Frank, do you think it's some of Reverend Sanders' men?" Katie wrung a dishtowel with her hands, nearly tearing it.

"I don't know. But I will find her." Frank looked thoughtful. "Was she wearing her loadout vest?"

"Yes. I'm sure of it."

"Good. If she isn't too badly injured, she may be able to help us find her."

Katie looked confused.

'Remember those gadgets—the GoTennas—I bought to boost the cell signals? We had them wrapped up in the EMP blanket with the spare cell phones and radios."

"Yes, so?"

"I had her put a spare cell phone and one of the GoTennas in her loadout."

"Will she remember? Will they take it from her?"

"I don't know, but it's the best we can hope for. You all get moving. I'll take that old truck I borrowed at the camp."

"Mr. Lowman?"

"Yes, Eli?"

"I would like to come with you. The others can bug out without me, but you should not go alone."

Frank thought a minute. "OK. Move your gear to the other truck and I'll get mine."

After kissing a tearful Katie good-bye and getting the others loaded and on the move, Frank grabbed his loadout vest, AR-15 and gear and met Eli at the truck. "It looks like they went toward Gaylesville."

Eli eyed the loadout vest. "Mr. Frank, do you have another one of those?"

"I should have thought of that Eli, hold on." Frank went back to the main trailer. Soon he was back with a second vest, another AR-15 and a .40-cal Springfield semiautomatic pistol that matched his own. "These are Katie's spares. You may have to adjust the straps."

Frank helped him adjust it, then they loaded the truck: a three-day emergency food pack, STOMP pack, sleeping bags, a case of AR-15 ammo, a couple extra boxes of .40-caliber ammo and a two-man tent. In his backpack, Frank had two sets of camo BDUs, several changes of underwear and socks and a toiletry kit. Finally he tossed in his HAS (hunting and snaring) bag, which, according to Max, "has everything needed to hunt, fish and snare." Frank never again wanted to be on the road without being fully prepared.

Frank tossed the keys to Eli. "You drive. I'll scan the road with the binoculars."

"Yes, sir, Mr. Frank." He snatched the keys midair and got in the driver's side. "I'll bet whoever it is won't head toward Birmingham. Too much heat and too many roadblocks."

"So we head toward Rome?"

"The only other option is toward Huntsville or Fort Payne." He thought for a moment. "Reverend Sanders' men aren't welcome in Fort Payne, and both Huntsville and Birmingham have strong military presence. I say toward Rome."

Frank took out one of the spare cell phones that was paired with another of the GoTennas and activated it. The small map on the phone's screen was clear of any signals.

AL9, Northeast Alabama

Somewhere between Gaylesville, Alabama, and Rome, Georgia, on Alabama 9, Max came to as the car bounced over debris in the road. Disoriented, she didn't understand how she went from being on watch at the OP to being bounced around the backseat of a car.

"Well, look who decided to wake up."

The voice was unpleasant, and unfamiliar. "Maybe I should introduce myself. I am William Wright. I know your father."

Max recognized the name from her father's story of getting home from New York. She could feel the sticky wetness of blood on the side of her head. The throbbing pain each time the car hit a bump told its own story. "What the hell is going on?"

"I do like someone who gets to the point. We both do, don't we, Clara?"

"Sure, whatever."

Max could tell Clara wasn't too pleased, whoever the hell she was.

"Your dad made a big mistake, pissing me off the way he did. Yes, sir, a big mistake."

"Look, just let me go. I won't tell him it was you." Talking made Max's head throb worse; the pain was nearly blinding.

"Oh, we are beyond that. I *want* him to follow. I owe him, and I am going to get even."

"Look, aren't things screwed up enough?"

"You know, I don't care. Your dad and I have a date with destiny. I know that sounds trite, but so be it."

He held up the GoTenna and the cell phone he'd removed from her vest while she was unconscious. "If I'm not mistaken, I believe if I turn this on, your dad will come right to me."

Max tried not to look surprised he knew about the GoTenna.

"I can see you are surprised. I saw this thing on Facebook, and wondered what fools would buy such crap. Now I know."

"We'll be out of range." Max tried to discourage him. "It only goes a couple miles."

"Then we better turn it on. Don't want ol' Frank to lose us."

He turned on the cell phone and then the GoTenna, bringing up the GoTenna application on the phone. The small cell phone screen soon showed an even smaller map with a blip and identifier, showing Frank's location near the edge of detection.

"Hi, Frank!" Bill sounded cheerful.

* * *

Several miles back, Frank smiled as the blip and identifier showing Max's unit blinked on. "Got you, you son of a bitch!" He clapped Eli on the shoulder. "He's just a couple of miles ahead. Turn off 35 onto 9."

Frank wondered, of course, why Willie wasn't taking a direct route. Maybe he was avoiding blockades and army checkpoints.

* * *

"OK, I think *that's* enough inducement."

With a wicked grin, Bill turned off the GoTenna and cell.

* * *

In Frank and Eli's truck, Frank swore. "We must be out of range; lost the signal."

He consulted the map in his lap. "Looks like there aren't any roads for them to turn off on. Keep on this heading."

"Yes, sir, Mr. Frank." Eli didn't take his eyes from the road.

* * *

Ahead of them by six miles, Bill pointed at a driveway ahead on the left.

"Pull in there. Go as far as you can from the road."

"What if he *catches* us?" Clara asked, turning in on the designated driveway. The drive meandered through a meadow and ended behind an old barn, once a glorious red but now faded and collapsing.

"Park here."

Bill indicated they should stop out of sight behind the barn. "If he stops, we'll just have to have our little party before I wanted to."

He smiled as he fondled Max's AR-15. He figured fifteen minutes was long enough. "OK, let's get back on the road, but no hurry. Let them get ahead a ways."

Clara looked right and left nervously as she entered the highway, and she kept glancing at the mirror.

"Holy shit, Clara," Bill said with a sneer. "They *are* ahead of us."

She let out a breath she hadn't realized she was holding. "You must be right."

"There, see," he cackled. "Clever Frank is rushing to catch up to us, while we mosey along behind him."

* * *

Frank and Eli peered ahead, seeking any sign of a vehicle, to no avail.

"Damn it. They couldn't be that far ahead of us or moving that much faster," Frank said, smashing his fist into the old pickup's dash, cracking the worn naugahyde.

"Maybe they pulled into a driveway and just let us pass," Eli suggested.

"That would mean he knows about the GoTenna. I don't think he's that smart."

But Frank couldn't shake his doubts. After another few minutes of pushing the old truck at top speed with no results, Frank decided Eli was right.

"God, I hate Willie! I never hated anyone before. Turn around. Let's go back and check a few driveways."

"Willie? The same Willie from New York?"

"Yes, Eli. The same. I didn't want to scare Katie but the track I found matches the ones we found from Willie. I doubt anyone from around here can afford those shoes he wears."

Eli did a precise three-point turn and headed back.

* * *

"Hmmm. Think they figured out we skunked them yet?" Bill smirked at Max. "Babe, pull into the next promising drive."

"Call me *babe* again and you'll be walking," Clara said grimly, as she pulled into what appeared to be an overgrown driveway, but actually was a non-maintained farm road.

"Well, well, well. An unmarked road! Let's see where it goes."

Bill reminded Max of the latest incarnation of *Batman*'s Joker.

Reaching the second turn on the farm road paralleling the highway, Clara fought with the wheel to keep the car on the ruts. Another few miles and the condition deteriorated until they were threatened with high-centering the car between ruts. "We have to get back on the road!"

Clara was having difficulty controlling the car at anything above a crawl.

"There—" Bill indicated another overgrown washboard road, seeming to go in the direction they needed. "It goes back on the highway."

Clara turned onto it. Just when she was sure she'd lose a tooth from the jarring, they reached two posts and a rusty-padlocked chain blocking the road.

"Drive though it!" Bill ordered.

Seeing no way around, Clara gunned the engine, smashing into the logging chain at nearly twenty miles per hour. Lucky for them the rusty padlock gave way almost immediately.

"*Yahoo-oo,*" Bill chortled, giving a rebel yell—at least his impression of one.

To Max it sounded like someone choking a coyote.

"Give it a few minutes, then turn on the GoTenna."

"Honey, please. Let's just get to Atlanta and stop this cat-and-mouse stuff."

Clara wasn't sure who was cat and who was mouse, and she didn't want to find out.

"OK, Clara. We'll goose old Frank one more time, then full speed for Atlanta."

* * *

Eli and Frank just missed seeing the entry, driving right by it in their haste to find Willie. A few miles down the road, Frank had Eli turn around again and head back towards Rome.

Lowman Caravan

"You sure you won't come, George?" Katie asked the old widower who had been so instrumental in helping Earl and Frank get to the BOL one more time.

"Naw. I can't abide sittin' on this wounded thigh. I'll jus' watch the place for ya. I don't think them army fellows will bother an old man much with you folks gone. Nice that I have no real clue where ya'll going, ain't it?" He smiled and laughed a little.

"OK, George. Just don't do anything foolish."

"Don't worry, Katie. I'll be as harmless an old man as possible."

With regret she pulled away, watching George wave good-bye as they drove down the gravel drive toward County Road 114 to Gaylesville. Katie hoped they wouldn't run into the army patrol sent to bring them in. Because the general had directed them by way of Florence, the road to Waleska should be clear. At least she hoped so.

To say Katie was distracted would be understatement. After nearly hitting a stalled car, she asked Marlene to drive, as her worry for Max's safety was making her ignore road hazards.

"Don't worry, Katie. Frank and Eli will find her safe and sound." Marlene tried to comfort her friend as they switched positions.

"Marlene, we don't know that. What if some creep like that Willie has her? From what Frank told me, he's capable of anything."

"Well, worry never solv't anythin', and while the lad is acting the maggot, if two men *can* solve it, it'll be Frank and Eli," Marlene said, her Irish accent thickening in her own worry.

"Marlene's right, Katie," Earl said from the back. "Frank will get her back, and if that git Willie has her, Max will give him a run for it."

For the next few miles, conversation lagged as Katie, Marlene, Earl and David pondered what might happen to Max. Outside of Adairsville, Marlene stopped the car on a hilltop.

"Do you all see what I'm looking at," she asked.

"Sure looks like a roadblock," Katie said, peering through the dirty windshield.

"And it doesn't appear to be police or military," David said, lowering the binoculars he'd pulled from the bug-out bag, "Bunch of yahoos in camo. Rifles and side arms don't match, and their grooming is all over the map."

"I don't get a good feeling about this—"

A knock on the glass startled them all.

Outside, several men in camo, their guns trained on the car, signaled that they should roll down the window.

"And what do you fine fellows want," Marlene asked through a partly lowered window.

"Please lay all weapons on the floor of the car and step out. This vehicle is being confiscated."

One man, in front of the others and wearing a black armband, seemed to be the leader.

"We will not! Let us through—"

Raising his side arm, a Ruger 9 mm, the leader fired into the air. "I said, drop your weapons to the floor of the vehicle and get out!"

He lowered the weapon and pointed it at Marlene.

Earl started to raise his weapon, bristling at someone pointing a loaded gun at his wife. A shot from one of the other men crazed the glass of the rear window and barely missed him. Needing no further encouragement, all four complied and soon stood outside their vehicle, hands in the air. Two rough-looking men patted them down, more thoroughly than required for Marlene and Katie, leaving them shaken and disgusted. When Earl complained, one of the guards threated to pistol-whip him.

"Under what authority are you confiscating our vehicle and supplies?" Katie was furious.

"Just shut up," the leader said curtly. "You'll find out all you need to know at the camp."

They watched morosely as one of the hoodlums drove away with all their arms, supplies and hopes.

An ancient, gold-colored, twelve-passenger van pulled up. Before they could board, their hands—except for David's—were tie-wrapped together.

"Is this really required?" Marlene was indignant. "You've taken our weapons and patted us down."

"Shut up or you'll be tasting duct tape."

The drive to the camp was mercifully short, as it wasn't comfortable sitting on the sprung seats of the decrepit van with their hands tie-wrapped behind their backs. David grimaced in pain as every bottoming of the worn suspension jarred his wounded shoulder.

The camp was at a former tire plant outside Rome, Georgia. The property was fenced and had one large, abandoned industrial building from the 1940s. A hodge-podge of tents, from large canvas to single pup, dotted the landscape. There were also porta-potties and a mess tent. The van stopped at a large tent with a crudely lettered sign in front that said PROCESSING.

The driver smirked as he opened the door and said, "Welcome to the People's Militia of Rome."

AL9, Near the Georgia-Alabama Border

Bill scowled. "I do *not* care. Just pee your pants."

"OK, but this is your car," Max said.

"Bill, stop," Clara begged. "I don't want to smell piss all the way to Atlanta."

"If they catch up, I will kill them. You understand that, don't you, Max?"

"So you say. That doesn't change the fact I have to pee."

Bill pulled the car to the roadside. "Clara, go with her. Wouldn't want her getting lost."

Clara opened the door and let Max out, holding on her the .38-caliber revolver with which she'd shot Reverend Sanders.

"You try anything, sweetie," Clara smiled, "and I will kill you."

Clara marched Max to a clump of bushes with a few small saplings. "OK, pick a tree and do your business." She gestured at the limited cover the bushes provided.

With a look of disgust, Max unfastened her jeans and, leaning back against a tree, lowered them and squatted. On the ground beside the tree was a three-foot limb about half as big around as her wrist. Looking straight ahead, Max grabbed the limb as she stood up. She swung it as hard as she could, catching Clara on the side of the head and knocking her to the ground.

Taking off like a frightened deer and fastening her pants on the run, Max crashed deeper into the woods. Behind her, Bill's rage-filled bellowing and the crack of wild pistol shots creasing through the brush faded as she ran deeper into the East Alabama pines and scrub.

Torn between chasing Max and inspecting Clara's injuries, Bill elected to check on Clara first. The limb had opened a large gash on her cheek, and the side of her head was covered in blood. After a long, tense moment, she blearily opened one eye.

"Shit, that hurts," she said thickly. "Did the bitch get away?"

"Yes."

Bill helped her stand. When he let go, she nearly fell. He helped her to the car.

"We have to get going— Can't chase her—" Clara mumbled, as she sank onto the passenger seat.

With Clara injured, Bill would have to chase Max on his own, leaving Clara by herself, which would be disastrous if Frank were to show up.

"Damn it!" He slammed the door to the car, making Clara wince in pain.

Bill got in on the driver's side. Reaching over to the GoTenna and cell phone, he switched them on. Bill turned back on the road to drive to Atlanta, knowing Frank would follow the signal. Bill hoped he could stay ahead.

* * *

Frank looked at the cell phone when it reacquired the signal from the other GoTenna and beeped.

"There they are again!"

Unlike before, the signal stayed steady.

"But is it Max?" Eli asked. "Or is Willie leading us on, Mr. Frank?"

"Good question," Frank said as he accelerated the truck as fast as he dared. Above seventy the steering wheel shook and the entire truck shuddered from unbalanced tires.

* * *

Hearing Willie and Clara's car drive off, Max headed toward the road. She felt the various pockets of her loadout vest, disappointed to find all its compartments empty. That bastard must have had fun searching her while she was unconscious. Max had almost felt sorry for Willie when her father told about kicking him out of that New York City hotel. Whatever pity she'd felt vanished with each painful throb of her head. Max peered out of the woods to the road just in time to see the old truck roar past, glimpsing Eli in the passenger seat.

Great, she thought, *What do I do now?*

Headquarters

Birmingham FEMA Center

"General, it is *unsatisfactory* that all you found was *one old man!*"

The president was livid.

"Sir, I sent a patrol as soon as you ordered me to. They must have been tipped off."

"Well, duh, General. What gave you a clue?" The president paced behind his desk. "What did this *old man* have to say about their destination?"

"Speaking personally, sir, he was a bit addled. He kept repeating that they left him, and wouldn't tell him anything."

"How persuasive were you?"

"Well, I didn't waterboard him but we grilled him for several hours."

The sarcasm was lost on the president.

"Maybe you should have. Can I speak with him?"

"Sir, he was so distraught we felt it best not to detain him. He'll be there if we need him. The only vehicle was a DeSoto with a burned-out engine."

"I want a thorough canvas of nearby relatives. It's not like they can check into a damn Holiday Inn."

"Already in progress. A second daughter lives near Rome. A patrol is heading there now."

"Keep me appraised." The president turned and glared out the window.

General Pratt saluted and departed. The intercom on the president's desk chimed as the general left and the president almost broke it slamming the button down. "Yes?"

"Sir, the secretary of state needs to talk to you about California."

"Damn. Alright, send him in."

The secretary of state, George Daily, formerly a State Department staffer on vacation fishing on the Alabama coast when the EMP hit, stepped in. The previous secretary of state had been on the same Middle East trip as the VP and was presumed to be a pile of radioactive ash somewhere in Tel Aviv along with the vice president.

"Well?" The president glowered at him as he'd glowered at General Pratt.

George seemed to shrink but, to his credit, didn't flee. "Sir, we have more reports of Chinese landing supplies and troops in San Francisco. They've taken Taiwan and EMP-ed Japan. There are unconfirmed reports of additional landings in San Diego and Seattle."

"Damn it! Fucking vultures." He sat dejectedly. "What assets do we have in California?"

"Sir, most of those bases were shut down or reduced to maintenance staffing levels. With all the cutbacks, frankly, not much."

President Wright recalled all those budget meetings where he and his Congressional cronies had voted to reduce the military. He sighed. This was not supposed to happen. He looked up at Secretary Daily. "Anything else?"

"We have lost contact with our bases in Alaska and all listening stations across the Arctic."

"The EMP?"

"No, sir. They were reporting in yesterday. Today we can't raise them."

"OK, brief the senior staff but no one else."

"Yes, sir."

As the secretary of state made his exit, President Wright closed his eyes, massaging his temples. He had no clue what to do next. He'd recalled all overseas troops, and now every piss-ant country previously holding back because of US troops was having a field day decimating their neighbors. The entire world was going crazy.

Processing Tent

The People's Militia of Rome

"If you work hard, you will be treated fairly. We will provide food, water, medical care, a cot and three square meals a day. If you *don't* do what you're told, there will be repercussions."

The tall, lean man—called "The Brigadier" by his militia—took the evil-smelling cigar from his mouth. "These men will tell you where you are to go, and what your duties will be."

Katie was getting angrier by the minute. They had separated Marlene and her from David and Earl, taking David to the hospital tent because of his wound and Earl to be assigned "men's work." Marlene and she were assigned "women's work": cooking and laundry. The looks some of the militia regulars had given them as they were marched to the cooking tent made her wonder what else was included in women's work. She didn't want to find out.

On their way to the mess tents she couldn't help but notice a large number of golden chanterelle mushrooms that appeared to be growing wild all over the camp; it gave her an idea.

The lead cook, a wizened ex-army mess sergeant, assigned her to cut up vegetables for venison stew. Actually, they hadn't had much luck with venison since the first week or two, so it was more of a stray pet stew. Katie tried not to think of the ingredients.

"Hey, Cooky . . . !" Katie called.

He'd insisted they call him Cooky; she doubted he remembered his original name.

"What you want, newbie?"

He pushed the worn ball cap he habitually wore back on his bald pate. He seemed friendly, and Katie wondered how he had fallen in with the militia.

"I noticed some chanterelle mushrooms on the way over. We could add some to spice this up a little."

"I don't cotton to that fancy stuff."

"I'll eat some in front of you. You can trust me."

"OK, fine. Go get a few and show me."

He signaled a guard, who followed her out to an untrammeled area near the fence, where she quickly picked a pound or so of fresh golden chanterelles, looking like little golden trumpets with fluted sides. She carried them back using the bottom of her tee shirt as an apron. Back at the mess tent, she laid them out for Cooky to examine. He cautiously lifted one to his nose and sniffed.

"Well, don't that beat all. Smells like peaches."

"Sautéed with butter they taste peppery, and they add a nice pepper note to stews."

"Eat a couple."

He looked at her skeptically.

She grabbed one of the larger ones and, after rubbing off the dirt and rinsing it, ate it, savoring the fruity aroma and peppery taste of fresh mushroom. She did the same with a second.

After fussily checking all she'd brought back—and tossing a few with ragged edges and touches of rot—he scowled approval to add them to the women's stew.

The women's stew was made with inferior cuts of meat. "Can't have you poisoning the men," he said, before rushing over to yell at a young girl who had dropped a pan of grease.

"Are those really safe?" Marlene asked when Cooky couldn't hear.

"Of course."

Katie smiled.

Atlanta, Georgia

The aging truck couldn't keep up with Bill and Clara's car.

Bill kept the GoTenna activated and stayed enough ahead that they could barely see Frank's signal. A couple times, they outpaced the unit's range and had to slow to keep them synced.

On the outskirts of Atlanta's warehouse district, Bill turned the GoTenna and cell phone completely off. "Let the games begin," he said with a grin.

Clara didn't answer. She'd fallen asleep, which worried Bill.

He swerved around stalled and wrecked cars, trying to make good time as he penetrated further into Atlanta's heart. He could see smoke rising from several burned-out skyscrapers. The ones that hadn't burned had their windows knocked out for ventilation. Bill didn't want to know how hot those concrete and steel boxes could get in a Georgia summer sun, especially with intact windows and no air conditioning.

Atlanta looked like a war zone—bodies festering in the heat and humidity that was summertime Atlanta. Flies everywhere. Pillaged goods as flat-screen TVs and expensive game systems lay about like discarded toys. Bill figured the looters realized early that electronics were useless without electricity.

They passed one shopping center where a convoy of burned Army and National Guard supply trucks smoldered. Bodies dressed in camo BDUs were strewn about like broken dolls. The streets were empty but Bill felt eyes watching him. A tattered RATION DISTRIBUTION CENTER sign hung listlessly in the still, hot air, one side loose from its support.

Bill was glad Clara was asleep; she'd make him turn around and leave if she saw all this.

He felt like he was where he belonged. He searched for an empty warehouse, one large enough to hide the car and lay in wait for Frank.

Near Mile Marker 2

Alabama State Route 9

Max thought about returning to the BOL, but decided she'd be better off heading for her sister Martha's place. She didn't want to be intercepted by Army or National Guard patrols and taken to a FEMA camp. She took stock: sturdy boots with extra-long paracord laces, one paracord survival bracelet. Under the insole of her left boot were credit card–sized survival kit metal plates that included fish hooks, arrow heads, a small saw, line locks and other useful small tools. Under the insole of her right boot were two tightly folded space blankets.

    She felt sure with the skills learned by attending wilderness survival courses that she could make it in a couple days if she avoided other people. She moved further into the woods, away from the road, and started hunting the proper types and sizes of wood she'd need. She considered fashioning a primitive bow and arrow but decided she'd be better at snares and fishing. She also wanted a handle for the saw blade. As she walked, she watched for edible mushrooms, and snacked on a few.

    At an abandoned campsite she found a few plastic bottles with lids and a couple aluminum cans, which she placed in a discarded plastic grocery sack. By sun position, she judged it was near noon. The air was still and smelled of pine. Although it was cool in the shade she was being eaten alive by mosquitoes.

At a small stream she smeared her face, hands, and all exposed skin with a thin coating of red Alabama clay. The mud would keep the worst biters away even if it made her look like a refugee from *Naked and Alone*. She followed the stream to where it joined a larger creek. She stopped and listened intently; all she heard was water, birds and small forest animals. She sniffed the air—no trace of campfire smoke or other human smells that her weak, human nose could discern.

She decided it was safe to rest for a bit, and maybe catch a fish for lunch.

Removing the paracord bracelet, she unraveled it to full length. After both long leads were unraveled she had about eight feet of paracord. Using the sharp edge from the toolkit, she cut off one melted end of the paracord, revealing the inner cords. She cut off the other melted end and then teased out two internal cords, leaving the rest. She wanted to seal the ends by searing them but that would wait until she had a fire. Tying the two inner cords together with an Albright bend, she now had a line of roughly sixteen feet. She separated one of the fishhooks from the survival card and tied it onto one end of the sixteen-foot line with a barrel knot. Finding a proper-size sapling, she used the small saw to cut and strip it of branches and leaves.

With the line attached to the narrow end, it made a serviceable fishing pole.

At creek side she turned over rocks until she found larva and nymphs for bait. Walking along the creek, she found a place where a boulder created an eddy. Threading a nymph onto the hook, she carefully dropped it upstream of the rock. With care she used the pool to guide the bait into the eddy. She was actually surprised when she felt the tug of a strike! She gave a short jerk to set the hook, and then lifted a nice twelve-inch trout from the stream. She quickly dropped it on the ground and killed it with a rock. Using the same type of nymph, and moving down the bank to other eddies, she soon had three trout. Taking from her sack one of the plastic bottles—one that according to its label had previously held water—she filled it with creek water and put it, and the fish, back in the sack.

In a nearby clearing, she scraped a circular area free of dry pine needles and leaves, and set up a small pile of dried moss and pine needles. She set the water bottle in full sunlight—the UV radiation from the noon sun helped kill microorganisms.

From her sack of cans and bottles she pulled an empty soda can and, using fine clay and a little water, polished the concave end until it was bright and shiny. Positioning the can bottom carefully, she focused the midday sun's rays onto the pile of tinder. It took a few seconds but soon a small wisp of smoke curled up from the moss. Max gently blew on the ember catching in the moss until a small flame erupted, and then she judiciously fed pine needles, then small sticks, and finally larger sticks, until she had a hot fire going. She hoped the smell wouldn't draw undo attention. Using the small saw she cut off the top of a soda can, rinsed it and filled it with water. She placed the water-filled can in the center of the fire.

With the same tool that had the saw edge, she used the opposing blade edge to gut the trout, tossing the offal into the creek. Using green twigs she propped open the trout, and then ran through them lengthwise a green branch about as big around as her little finger. Sitting by the fire, she used the branches to hold the fish over the coals, turning them occasionally to make sure they cooked evenly. When the water boiled she used a green leaf to protect her hand as she pulled the can from the fire and set it aside to cool.

By the time the trout were cooked the water was cool.

She ate one fresh-cooked trout and drank the muddy-tasting water. When she was done she refilled the can and placed it onto the coals. After the can boiled again, she again set it aside to cool. Using some ash, she halfway filled another aluminum can from which she had removed the top and bent down the sharp edges, making a primitive firesafe. She dropped some glowing coals inside and packed more ash around and on top of them, sealing the can with a wad of moss. She then slid the previously removed top back on to secure everything in place. She doused the fire with water from the creek. Taking a second bottle that had also held water before, she carefully poured the cooled water into it. She wrapped the other two cooked trout in wild grape leaves and placed them, the firesafe, and the water bottle into her sack.

She was ready to begin her journey.

Warehouse District

Atlanta

Frank knew they were being played. Each time the dot on the cell phone faded out, it would mysteriously reappear, egging them on. If Willie didn't know they were following, it was obvious he would have left them behind over an hour ago.

"Eli, I think you are right. He knows about the GoTenna and is using it to lead us into a trap."

"I hate to be right this time, Mr. Frank."

"We have little choice. But now that we know it's a trap we can take precautions."

"Yes. We can perhaps become the trappers."

Reaching the Atlanta outskirts, Frank swore as the blip showing Willie's—and presumably Max's—position again winked out.

"Damn it. That's the old warehouse district. It'll be cat-and-mouse in there finding them."

"You are right. I remember this area was not safe several years ago. I'm sure it is even worse now."

"You have a penchant for understatement, Eli."

Frank eyed the smoldering buildings and abandoned cars. Picturing his little girl—he thought of her as such even though she was twenty-six—with that monster Willie in this ruin of a city was driving him mad with worry.

"If he wants us to find him, I'll bet he'll be within a couple blocks of the last GoTenna coordinate." He looked out the window at the remains of the National Guard distribution center. "And this is it."

"We should hide the vehicle and proceed on foot."

Eli matched actions to words as he pulled into an alley and then into an open garage door for an abandoned machine shop. Parking the car, he jumped out and pulled the screeching door closed behind them. Frank winced at all the noise.

"OK, here—" he handed Eli a Cobra CX115 FRS transceiver—"go to channel 16. The radios are encrypted for that frequency." Frank set his radio and paired it to Eli's. They slung their AR-15 MBRs over their necks using single-point slings, and allowed the rifles to hang on their backs. Each had a harness, with two additional thirty-round magazines of 5.56 NATO for the MBRs, and extra .40-caliber magazines for their pistols.

"Let's go to the roof if we can, and get the lay of the land."

Eli led Frank to stairs into the building's dark interior. From his harness Frank pulled out a headlamp and a flashlight. He handed the flashlight to Eli and put the headlamp on. As they climbed they kept their heads on a swivel and listened for odd noises. Each clutched their .40-cal Springfield semi-automatic pistols at low ready position and used single hand signals to communicate.

They sighed in relief when they reached the door to the roof without incident.

The padlock on the roof was only a momentary delay. Frank watched dumfounded as Eli produced a lock pick set and deftly opened it.

"Don't leave home without them," Eli said with a smile as he opened the door, nearly blinding them with daylight after the interior gloom.

From the roof, Atlanta's skyline devastation was even more apparent. The once proud city showed numerous ruins from out-of-control fires triggered by the EMP, as well as arson and riots that followed. Entire neighborhoods had been reduced to burned-out basements and crumbling brick walls. The air was thick with the stench of raw sewage and wet ash. From their coign of vantage they spotted several buildings large enough to hide vehicles, and recorded them on notebooks, which were part of the loadout vests' inventory.

"Alright, if you take that side, and I take this one, we can cover twice the territory. If you find them, click twice on the radio and wait. I will do the same. Move to a safe location, radio the position, and we move in together."

"Yes, Mr. Frank, a good plan. Stay safe."

They gingerly retraced the stairs.

As they reached the ground floor, a voice called out: "Put down your weapons, we have you surrounded."

The ominous sound of a pump action shotgun being cocked punctuated the words.

"This building belongs to the Soldiers of the Prophet. You are trespassing."

Eli, realizing he was dealing with fellow Muslims, hoped Frank would be quiet and play along. "Peace be with you brother," Eli said loudly with a smile. "I claim the right of guests." "Surely you have read the Qur'an Surah 51: 24–27?"

A tall black man with an acne-ravaged complexion stepped into a beam of light from the dirty ground-floor windows. "And who are you to ask for such?"

"Surely in these dark times fellow followers of the Prophet must succor each other against the heathens."

"And this kafir with you?" He gestured at Frank with the business end of a sawed-off Remington 12-gauge.

"He is my ma malakat aymanukum. I spared him his life, and in return he serves me."

"Peace be upon you then. Come." Two more men came in from the shadows, one armed with an AK-47 with redwood furniture, and the other an AR-15.

"May we retrieve our weapons?" Eli asked.

"We will bring them."

Eli knew better than to argue.

The guards herded them into a nearby structure. Inside the smells were of unwashed bodies, spices, and the musty odor of an old building. In a large room there were several couches, and pillows strewn about the floor.

"Sit. We will bring food and drink as is proper according to Qur'an, and you will tell me why you are *visiting* us."

Eli and Frank sat on one of the couches. Their guards didn't sit, didn't smile and would not make eye contact. In a few minutes women, fully dressed in the hajib, with full face coverings as well, brought in platters with cooked squab and samovars of hot tea.

"Eat. Then tell me why I should treat you as guests and not invaders."

Their host sat with crossed arms and watched as they each took a squab and ate, and drank the strong, fragrant tea.

"It is good to see even in this heathen land that there is one who knows the proper ways. Praise be upon you, and upon Allah," Eli said, wiping bird grease on his sleeve.

"And peace be upon you. Now, what brings you here?"

"I seek my man's daughter. She was forcefully taken by the lowest of kafirs. We followed them to near here until we lost them. We were searching for them when you found us."

"Inshallah. I am Mohammed Rahman. I will treat you as guests, and you may go in peace. But if you betray this trust, I will kill you." He signaled to one of the guards, who left and then returned with their weapons, which had been unloaded and the magazines removed.

"Do not load these until you have left my home. Finish your meal and then please leave."

He stood and left the room, followed by his guards.

* * *

While Frank and Eli parlayed, Bill drove in circles looking for an appropriate building. Finally he spotted one with a pull-up garage door. Clara was still asleep, which still worried him, but they needed to get off the street. The feeling of being watched was almost physical.

The door was padlocked but a well-placed hit with a section of rebar broke the cheap lock. Bill was grateful someone had oiled the door mechanism. It rattled and screeched only moderately as he raised the door. The interior, dimly lit by a few dirty windows, looked empty. Bill pulled the car in and ran the door down behind them.

Clara looked bad. The entire side of her face was bruised and swollen where Max had hit her with the branch. She looked half-Klingon, Bill thought.

Damn it! He should have gone with Clara. Then they would still have Max. At least it appeared that Frank still thought they had her. After all, he was still following them.

After unloading supplies and unrolling a sleeping bag, he carefully lifted Clara from the passenger seat and laid her on the warehouse floor. Using a washcloth and bottled water, he wiped the blood from her hair. He tenderly applied antibacterial cream to the gouge made by the branch.

Through all his ministrations she barely stirred, which worried him even more. His rage built, blaming Frank and his hell-spawned daughter for his problems, forgetting he had kidnapped Max in the first place.

After he did everything possible to make Clara comfortable, he went out to reconnoiter. Without Clara, he would have to be doubly cautious when he lured Frank into the final confrontation.

The building had the pull-up door, one entrance in the front and one entrance in the alley. Bill figured Frank would choose the stealthy route and use the alley, so he studied it minutely. With a little stealth of his own, he could really surprise Frank.

* * *

After leaving Mohammed's building, Eli and Frank loaded and checked their weapons.

"I am sorry, Mr. Frank."

"Why, Eli? You probably saved our lives."

"That may be. But I still showed you—who have showed me nothing but kindness—disrespect."

"Nonsense. Consider it over."

"It was good you stayed silent."

"I figured it was your play. You know more about Islam than I ever will."

"Inshallah, Mr. Frank. As Allah wills."

Eli and Frank split up to cover more territory, with Eli taking the street on one side of their shelter building and Frank taking the other. Periodic radio checks as they cleared buildings kept them appraised of each other's position.

Frank came abreast of a small building off by itself.

It had a single roll-up garage door, and a single entrance in front. And something had recently disturbed the rubbish in front of it, and a broken lock lay in the freshly disturbed area.

"Eli, come in . . ." Frank lowered the radio from his mouth.

"Yes, Mr. Frank."

"I am two blocks up. I think I have something and am checking it out . . ."

"Do you need me?"

"Not yet. I will check it out externally. Then if it is something, I will signal as we agreed. If you don't hear from me in ten, come running."

"10-4, Mr. Frank."

Frank stowed the radio in his vest's radio pocket and cautiously started around the side of the structure. Frank was suddenly sure he heard something.

He hated the nearly abandoned city almost as much as he had loved it when it pulsed with life. There—that fresh slide of rubble—the air was still, so it wasn't caused by wind. He quickened his pace, his combat boot–encased feet nearly silent.

There! Again a noise, closer this time. Find cover and wait, or go on and hope to outdistance whatever or whoever followed, that was the question.

Ahead was the dark entrance to an alley at the back of the building. Normally he would steer clear but now it was worth the risk. Ducking inside, he waited, holding his breath and quieting his rapidly beating heart.

The pursuer sauntered into view: a stupid cat!

In his instant of relief, Frank didn't notice a shadow move behind him in the recess of the alley. Without warning, a blow to the back of Frank's head dropped him to the ground, senseless.

*　*　*

Frank was unsure how much time had elapsed when he regained consciousness, squinting in the weak light. Pain seared through his head. He could feel his arms bound behind him and he was laying on his side. The sight that greeted him when he opened his eyes wasn't pleasant: Willie leered at him from an ancient wooden office chair.

"Willie—" Frank started.

"Bill. Please, call me Bill. I hate Willie."

Bill pointed the muzzle of Frank's own .40-cal Springfield at his face.

"I don't think you want to make me mad."

Frank could tell Bill was enjoying this.

"Willie—" Frank hated the pleading sound in his voice. "Bill!"

He pointed the deadly pistol directly at Frank's heart.

"Bill, I just want Max."

"Sorry, Frank, no can do. I shot her back on Alabama 9. And left her for the buzzards."

Frank felt the immediate dropping sensation of great loss. He closed his eyes tightly.

Bill enjoyed the horrified look that washed Frank's face at his lie. But he missed the follow-up rage that burned in Frank's eyes when he opened them. That would have required empathy, a quality that in Bill was in short supply.

Through his rage and grief, Frank tried to think.

"Bill, listen to me. I've come to take you to your father."

Frank felt sweat forming on his brow.

Willie's eyes were cold and filled with rage. "My father could care less."

Willie held the pistol higher, once again targeting Frank's head.

"He sent me. He is now the president."

Frank hoped the news would placate Willie.

"That doesn't change anything. *You* still owe me."

"*Owe* you? You tried to steal my car. You killed my daughter!"

Frank's own anger was rising.

"You threw me off the rider group."

"You refused to ride with someone who was armed. You seem to have overcome that."

"You both sound like children."

Clara, pushing up to her feet, came to stand shakily beside Willie.

She looked disgusted. "Bill, if he can take us to your father, you can get treated for your wounds. And we can stop running."

"Listen, Bill. I am sorry. We were all anxious about the EMP strike, about getting home. I acted rashly." Frank hoped his apology would get Willie to see Clara's logic.

For a moment it seemed Frank's words were having an effect. But only for a moment.

"Maybe I don't want to see my father and maybe I don't give a shit."

Frank could see Willie's finger tensing on the trigger. He closed his eyes.

They say if you hear the shot, then you aren't dead. In an enclosed space, the sound of a .40-cal report is deafening. Not believing that Willie had missed, Frank opened his eyes.

Willie was writhing on the floor, clutching his right hand. Clara was reaching for a revolver at her waist.

"I wouldn't do that if I were you, girl."

Frank recognized the African lilt to the voice.

Eli!

"You OK, Mr. Frank?"

Eli walked over and, while covering Clara with the pistol in one hand, cut the restraining tie from Frank's wrists.

"Other than a headache, yes, I am fine."

He rubbed his chafed wrists. "Nice timing, Eli."

Frank looked around for his pistol. It was laying a couple feet away, knocked from Bill's hand by Eli's precision shot. Frank worked the slide and checked that it still operated. Tucking it back in his holster, he went to Clara. After a thorough pat-down—and removing the .38-cal pistol tucked in Clara's waistband—Frank examined Willie's wrist.

Willie's right wrist was shattered and bleeding profusely.

From his loadbearing harness, Frank pulled a packet of quick clot and applied it to the wound. As the quick clot reacted with the blood to seal the wound, its temperature rose precipitously.

Willie howled with pain.

After the quick clot stopped the bleeding, Frank wrapped the wrist with an Israeli bandage and then secured Willie's hands. After searching Clara again, he also secured Clara's hands. By the time he was finished, it was getting dark.

"Eli, bring the truck here and we will spend the night. Tomorrow we take this asshole to Birmingham. Let his father deal with him."

"Yes, Mr. Frank. I am sorry about Max. She was the best."

Frank had pushed to the back of his mind Willie's claim that he'd killed Max on his way to Atlanta. Now it roared forth, almost blinding him with hurt and anger. He pulled the .40-cal from his holster and held it up to Willie's head. "Maybe Mr. President will have to take a corpse—"

"No, Mr. Frank! He is not worth it."

Eli reached toward Frank, knowing if he killed Willie it would bring nothing but trouble on the group.

"He lied."

Clara's simple statement silenced the two men.

"Go on." Frank's voice was cold.

His pistol, slightly shaking, was still trained on Willie's forehead. Frank's finger was tight on the trigger—a fraction of an ounce from sending Willie to hell.

"She clobbered me with a branch just before the Georgia border and escaped."

Frank could see the truth in her words from the wounds on her head. He sagged with relief and holstered his weapon.

Willie glared at her for exposing his lie. He had been enjoying Frank's misery, oblivious to how close he had come to death.

"Max is alive?" Frank's voice was barely above a whisper.

"Yes, sir. Please don't kill us." The pleading in her voice was genuine. "We last saw her around Mile Marker 2, on the Alabama side of the Rome highway."

"I am not a barbarian. I'm taking you both to Birmingham, where they can deal with you two officially."

"Are you sure you are OK, Mr. Frank?" Eli sounded concerned. "Maybe we should wait until morning to get the truck."

"No, I was only out for a few minutes. I don't think there is any permanent damage. Max is alive! And this piece of trash is going to the camp in Birmingham. He and his father are welcome to each other." He winced as he touched a bloody lump on the back of his head.

"Besides, we need the first aid kit to do a better job on Willie here. That quick clot may not be enough."

"OK, Mr. Frank. I will be right back."

Eli picked up his MBR and, slinging it over his shoulder, left the building.

"Why, Willie?" Frank asked. "What made you think stealing my car was such a good idea?"

Willie, sullen and silent, stared at the ground between his feet.

"Why chase me across the country? Kidnap my daughter? It doesn't make sense."

"I *didn't* chase you. We ended up in Atlanta completely by chance, and I got your address off a guy on a motorcycle. I figured it was time for payback, time for fate."

"You're lucky your old man is president. If he wasn't, you'd be dead."

Willie didn't answer. He just stared at the ground at his feet.

After making sure the prisoners were securely tied and mischief-proof, Frank searched their car. Inside he found MRE wrappers, trash and, most importantly, Max's loadbearing vest's contents, the GoTenna, her AR-15 and cell phone.

Frank turned his head to the sound of an approaching engine, oddly loud in the quiet of the ruined city. Soon lights flashed in the dirty windows on the roll-up door. Frank raised it and Eli drove the truck in beside Willie and Clara's car.

From the bed of the truck Frank grabbed the army surplus STOMP pack and went over to Willie.

While Eli covered him, Frank unbound Willie's arms and then did his best to debride the shattered right wrist. A .40-cal bullet does a lot of damage. After more than a few minutes work he was satisfied he'd done all he could.

Frank applied antibacterial cream and wrapped Willie's wrist with gauze. He then cut splint material to the right shape and splinted Willie's right hand. The splint was to keep him from tearing open the quick clot and bleeding to death. Finally, he wrapped the whole thing with an ACE bandage and then rebound Willie's hands.

"That's the best I can do. It should last until Birmingham if there are no delays," Frank said as he stood. He used bottled water to wash Willie's blood from his hands.

Next he saw to Clara's wound. A couple of butterfly bandages and she was patched up. Eli gestured that Frank should sit. "OK, Mr. Frank, it is your turn."

"But it isn't even bleeding much, Eli."

Frank winced as Eli cleaned the small gash and applied some ointment and a small bandage.

"Mr. Frank, you rest. I will take the first watch."

With drooping eyes, Frank let Eli take the first watch and settled into a fitful slumber. While he knew Max was well trained in survival techniques, it was still his baby girl in peril.

Presidential Chambers

Birmingham FEMA Camp

President Wright woke from a nightmare—he dreamed he was addressing the full Congress and realized he was naked. He hadn't had such a dream since he first ran for Congress. The China, Russia and Mexico issues would be enough to daunt any president. His concern for his son also warred for precedence in his mind. Was William a psychotic murderer? The evidence was there. William's mother had raised him spoiled, never lacking for anything, since the days when Wright had come into money.

  He couldn't believe how money had seemed to fall from the sky as soon as he was in the House. Well, fall from the sky if you didn't pay much attention to the source—or the ties—it came with. He remembered how terrified he'd been shortly before the EMP strike. He shivered, recalling the summons from the House Ethics Committee. How does one account for millions, when one's salary is less than two hundred thousand a year? Hypocritical bastards! They all did the same things. Some were just better at covering their asses. He guessed he got the last laugh.

  Of course, now all the money in the world was useless. All that mattered was where to get the next million gallons of oil or megawatts of electricity.

  Knowing he wouldn't sleep anymore, he swung his feet over the bed edge and pressed the call button on the bedside table.

  "Yes, Mr. President?"

"Get me some coffee. Bring it to the office."

"Yes, sir, Mr. President."

Wright dressed in comfortable clothes—blue jeans, a blue cotton shirt and loafers with no socks. As he exited his room, his escort of Secret Service and the naval attaché with the nuclear football—the case with the nuclear launch codes—followed. Wright wondered if the nuclear football was the same that President Paul had been saddled with or was it a new one just for him. A silly question because the late president's had been immolated along with him in the plane wreck.

At his office the Secret Service and attaché sat outside while he went in by himself.

On his desk was the latest intelligence briefing. The Chinese had moved as far as Sacramento and the surrounding fertile valleys. The Mexicans had poured across the southern borders and were pressing cities up and down Texas, California, Arizona and New Mexico. Nothing had been heard from the northern listening posts for days and shortwave broadcasts out of Alaska and Northern Canada talked about Russian invaders.

Formal diplomatic communiqués talked of humanitarian relief but Wright didn't buy it for one second. He turned to the report on military strength and deployment.

In spite of dire threats and warnings, AWOLs and desertions were at epic levels. Troops were disappearing almost as soon as they hit the ground. Anyone with a family that they loved seemed to disappear, especially if assignments came through that took them far away while no one looked after their loved ones at home. It seemed the only ones staying either had nowhere to go or weren't who you'd want to guard you anyway.

Oh, there were still some who placed duty and honor above all else, but sometimes Wright worried about them most of all. They seemed wound just a bit too tight. He made a few notes about possible troop deployments and considered re-targeting nukes to some of the cities being invaded, but he realized he did not want to be the president who nuked his own people.

How to strike the enemies so that they withdrew, without using troops or destroying that which he wanted to protect—that was the gist of his problem. Even if he were to launch an EMP strike, they'd see it and respond with full-fledged nuclear war.

At the bottom of the stack of briefings was a pile of documents he was supposed to go through as the new president, but he hadn't had much time for busy work. With a sigh he grabbed the stack and started reviewing all the supposed need-to-know information no longer relevant in a country without a working infrastructure. Then a file marked *Project Shiva* caught his eye and he tossed the other files back on the desk.

He just finished reading the complete file on Project Shiva when General Pratt was announced.

"Let him in. We have something to discuss. Oh, and get Cheyenne Mountain on the hook as well."

Camp

The People's Militia of Rome

In the women's tent in Rome, Katie was trying to talk quietly to Marlene.
"Marlene, wake up . . ." Katie hissed in Marlene's ear. Both had dropped into the cots, exhausted, after working all day and half the night in the mess tents.
"What, Katie?" Marlene protested sleepily. "You know we have to get up before sunrise—"
"Look, we need to find out where Earl is, and what they've done with David."
"David is still in the hospital tent. I saw him before I went to sleep. Not sure about Earl." She was more awake now.
"OK. We need to find him and get a message to him."
"Why?"
"I have a plan but we need a way to message him. Are they letting him see David?"
"I think so."
"That may be the way."
"What's up?"
"I'll let you know as soon as I have it all figured out. We have to get out of here."
"You said it! But with all these armed guards . . ."
"I think I can take care of them."
"Single-handedly? Just you by yourself?" Katie didn't mean to sound skeptical.
"A little help from mother nature."
With that last cryptic remark, Katie left Marlene's cot and crept back to her own.

It seemed only a second after Katie's head hit the flat pillow that she was awakened to head back to the mess tent. Cooky was already there. It seemed like he never left.

"Newbie, go get more of those mushrooms. The men loved them." He signaled the same guard to follow her as before.

She was soon back with more chanterelles. She grabbed some boletes as well.

She had to demonstrate that they were edible in the same way as before with the chanterelles. Some of the men were calling her the mushroom lady. She showed Cooky how to use mushrooms with powdered eggs and powdered cheese to make a half-decent omelet. Served with Yoder's canned bacon it was almost palatable.

"What's your name, newbie?"

Cooky was warming to her.

"Katie."

"Katie, you keep this up, you'll become one of us."

He smiled through teeth stained brown from years of coffee and cigarettes.

"I could gather more if Marlene, the women I came in with, could help."

"OK, done. But remember, if you try to escape you get assigned to the hospitality corps."

Katie wasn't sure what the hospitality corps was, but she was sure it wasn't good.

"Don't worry, escape isn't on my mind." *Yet*, she added silently.

As they gathered mushrooms, Marlene would bring those she wasn't sure of back to Katie for her approval. Some she rejected, some she allowed and others she asked where Marlene found them and marked it mentally for future purposes.

When they returned they had several pounds of edible bolete and chanterelle mushrooms. Cooky gave them lighter duties after they'd cleaned and sliced the mushrooms. Some went right into food being processed for lunch and the evening meal, some into solar desiccators for drying and later use.

Katie was pleased. Her plan was going well.

Marlene was confused and starting to get pissed. It seemed to her that Katie was bent on helping these yahoos when they should be escaping.

Just inside the Georgia Border

Max made good time that first day.

Taking a magnetized needle from the seam of one boot top, she used it and a small piece of dry-rotted wood to make a compass that floated in water in the palm of her hand. She would stop and sight her direction, each time choosing landmarks as far away as possible. She knew she could move faster on the road but it was more likely to be patrolled by people both good and bad. By the time the sun started to set she'd made about seven miles.

She found another good campsite on a creek near the river. The creek led to the Coosa and for the present she was following it. Game and fish were abundant by the river, and she had already added several useful items to her stash, including a tangled ball of fishing line, which she patiently untangled and wrapped around one of the cans as she walked. Soon she had a serviceable poacher's reel—a tin or aluminum can with a length of monofilament wrapped around it, a hook and weight. She planned on making good use of it.

From a cache of driftwood in a snag at one of the river bends, she found a walking staff, which could double as a bow.

Max set up camp as before, using coals from her firesafe to start a small fire. Using more paracord, she stretched out one space blanket to provide a cover and then used the other to wrap up pine needles to make a primitive mattress. Taking the leaf-wrapped trout from the pack, she laid them by the fire to warm while she refilled her water can and placed it over the fire to boil.

The monofilament she'd found was about ten-pound test. She knew that was too lightweight to be of use in a snare so she unwrapped three four-foot lengths from the can and then braided them together, using fire coals to seal the ends. With a combined strength of thirty pounds, it would work well for what she had in mind. Once the first length was ready, she clipped off three more and made a second braided monofilament. The first she made into a noose. It was nice the way the monofilament stiffened and stayed circular. She attached the other length to the loop, leaving a small leader to which the trigger would be attached. Seeing that the trout and water would take several minutes to get to temperature, she went back to a game trail she'd crossed that took advantage of a dry creek bed to get to the river. Using a bent-over sapling and fashioning a trigger by notching a couple twigs with the knife-edge, she set a snare.

Hopefully by morning she'd have something,

Returning to the fire, she found the trout piping hot and smelling wonderful. She wished she had salt and pepper and lemon, but hunger made a great sauce. Tomorrow she'd watch for wild onions or garlic, and maybe those chanterelle mushrooms her mom liked, to make the meal more flavorful. While she ate she set the now boiling water aside to cool.

Around the edge of the clearing she saw familiar wildflowers. After finishing off the second trout she checked the water. It was still pretty hot so she checked out the flowers. Sure enough, the miniature sunflowers on the six- to eight-foot stalks were jerusalem artichokes. Using a stick she dug up several of the starchy roots. They could be tasty if cooked like a potato. Tomorrow's dinner promised to be great.

Banking the fire so there would still be coals in the morning, she drank the muddy-tasting water. With any luck she'd find a larger jug and make a filter—where was a filter when you needed it! After reapplying slimy clay to her exposed skin to stave off mosquitoes and biting flies, she climbed onto her improvised mattress and was soon asleep.

* * *

It seemed she'd barely shut her eyes when light from the rising sun inserted itself between her eyelids. The golden morning light painted everything in warm hues, and the light morning breeze was soothing.

Max considered sleeping in as she rolled over, but the rustling and creaking from the improvised mattress and one particular twig poking her full bladder brought her completely awake, along with a bright wave of pain from her concussion, not to mention the realization of where she was and how she'd gotten there.

Climbing out of her improvised shelter, she stretched the crick out of her back. The river mists were beautiful and for a moment she forgot she was alone and miles from where she needed to be. With a sigh, she stretched her legs. She was sore after yesterday's hike, but at least her headache was nearly gone.

Max found a sturdy sapling and made an improvised toilet. Much relieved, she returned to her camp, where she unbanked the coals from the previous night's fire and loaded small twigs, then larger branches, onto it. Soon she had a nice fire. While it burned down to coals she checked her snare.

A medium-size rabbit was dead in the noose. She knew she'd have to watch for blow fly larva and other parasites and be sure to cook the meat completely, but her mouth watered at the thought of roast rabbit. She gutted and skinned the animal, peeling the skin like an old sock from the still-warm carcass. After tossing the offal into the river for the fish to eat, she carried the rabbit back to camp and laid the gutted rabbit near the fire. She took her poacher's reel to the river. After finding a couple grubs, she baited the hook and tossed the line out. It didn't take long to catch a few small fish, enough for breakfast. She rolled up her line and soon had the fish cooking over the fire.

She used green branches to spit the rabbit and set it roasting. Wrapping the jerusalem artichokes in several layers of green wild grape leaves, she placed them in the hot coals. She drank the rest of the water boiled the night before, careful not to disturb the layer of mud at the bottom. It was marginally better after settling all night. She rinsed out her can and refilled it to boil more. She turned the artichokes to cook evenly and monitored the fish and rabbit.

The fish finished first; she set them aside to cool. As before, it took a while for the water to boil. She turned the rabbit several times. She tested the rabbit, taking care not to burn her fingers, making sure it was cooked completely. When the haunch separated easily from the body she took it off the fire to cool. She let the artichokes cook for a good long time to be sure they were done.

After eating her fish, Max drank the tepid water and then put more on to boil to refill her water bottle. After the rabbit cooled she boned it as best she could and wrapped the meat with leaves to store in her sack. She couldn't resist eating one of the rear legs. It would have been better with salt, but it was still good.

After breakfast and preparing her walking lunch, she broke camp, loading coals into her firesafe and then dousing the fire. Folding and stowing her space blankets took longer than she expected. No matter how you tried, they never got as small as when new.

Checking her direction with her makeshift compass and setting a landmark, she was off.

Atlanta to Birmingham to Gaylesville

Eli and Frank took turns watching their prisoners; although it was largely unnecessary because Eli had retied them in such a way that struggling begot choking. Nonetheless, they didn't want to get caught unawares should anyone else stumble on their downtown Atlanta hideaway. Atlanta—once the Jewel of the South—was now a war zone between rival private factions, what remained of the police and the occasional National Guard patrol.

When the sun finally lit up the grimy windows Frank was ready to hit the road.

First, they had to move gear from the rear of the truck to the king cab, and, second, search Willie and Clara's car for useful items. They loosed Willie and Clara long enough to scarf down an MRE, drink water, and have a bathroom break. They then retied them and loaded Clara and Willie into the truck bed.

"Cover them up with that tarp," Frank said. "Keep the sun and dust off 'em."

"Let me do one thing," Eli said. "We don't want them alerting others; we don't need the attention."

Eli took a roll of duct tape and taped Willie and Clara's mouths, which earned him a hate-filled glare from each.

"Are you sure they'll be alright back there, Eli?"

Frank was concerned that Willie lived long enough to be returned to his father.

"It is still early. With any luck we'll be in Birmingham before it gets too hot." Eli smiled. "Besides, I think they earned their places."

Frank smiled back fiercely. "You're right, Eli."

Frank and Eli got into the front of the truck, this time Frank driving and Eli riding shotgun—or should it be called AR-15? They drove the deserted city streets, occasionally glimpsing a moving curtain or window shade, the few clues anyone still lived in Atlanta. At an intersection near where they'd first hidden their vehicle, Mohammed stood with arms crossed. They rolled down the window.

"Peace be with you," Mohammed said solemnly.

"And with you, my brother," Eli answered.

"Did you find the daughter of your man?" Mohammed peered into the truck.

"No. She escaped the infidel, who led us here hoping to kill us."

"Did you kill him?"

"No. We are returning him to a fate worse than death."

"Inshallah, go in peace."

"Inshallah. There is a working vehicle in the warehouse at the end of the block. Please take it as a gift." Eli waved and closed the window.

Frank let out a breath he didn't realize he was holding. "I am really, really glad you are with me, Eli."

"I am glad to be of service, Mr. Frank. He may have let you go."

"He might *not* have. Besides, without you, Willie would have killed me."

"Maybe so. As you Christians say, God works in mysterious ways, no matter what you call him."

"Inshallah," Frank said with a smile.

"Inshallah."

They threaded both deliberate and accidental roadblocks for several minutes until they found ramps onto I-20 heading east and west. What difference did it make now that there were no laws and no traffic? The eastbound side had fewer stalled and wrecked vehicles.

Even though many modern cars simply did an immediate reset when the EMP struck, the entire automobile still shut down. At sixty-plus miles per hour, the lose of power steering, power brakes and engine usually resulted in a collision.

Frank assumed fewer people wanted to head toward Augusta and the Barnwell federal nuclear facility across the river near Aiken, South Carolina. As they got further from Atlanta, out past Six Flags amusement park, the number of stalled and wrecked cars dropped off dramatically on the westbound side and they switched lanes at one of the crossovers that still bore the sign: WARNING OFFICIAL VEHICLES ONLY.

* * *

"Uh, General Pratt?" The non-com's voice sounded unsure.

"Yes, son, what is it," the general said, answering the intercom in his office.

"Sir, you better come out here. A Mr. Lowman says he has to talk with you."

"*Frank* Lowman?"

"Yes, sir."

"Hold him there. I'll be right out."

"Yes sir." The intercom went silent.

General Pratt donned his cap and, telling his secretary he'd be right back, left the command center. Walking briskly, he made the front gate in a few minutes, where Frank Lowman was standing near a beat-up, king-cab Ford Ranger, a tall black man beside him.

The guards were nervously handling their rifles, uncertain how to deal with this self-assured man.

"Frank, what can I do for you? You know you're taking a big risk; I'm supposed to arrest you on sight."

"I know, General. But before you do, you might want to see what I've brought you."

General Pratt came around the side of the truck and looked in the bed. With a flourish Frank jerked aside the tarp covering Clara and Willie.

"Well, I'll be damned!"

General Pratt stared in amazement at the two, who were still trussed-up like Thanksgiving turkeys, including duct-taped mouths. They blinked and ducked away from the sudden glare.

Frank untied Willie and Clara, who had to be helped out of the truck and could barely stand until the circulation in their arms and legs recovered.

Frank left their arms secured and the duct tape in place.

"Willie here shot himself while cleaning his gun." Frank looked the general straight in the eyes as he said this. "You better get him to the infirmary."

"Any charges you want to bring, Mr. Lowman?"

"Nope. Just a citizen doing his duty for his president."

"I'll see to it the president is informed of your actions."

"Then I can go?"

"Now hold on! My instructions were to bring you in for questioning about the whereabouts of one William Wright Junior. But by the looks of things, we've concluded that line of questioning."

The general reached out his hand and he and Frank shook. "Who is your friend?"

"This is Eli. Without his help we wouldn't be having this conversation. Eli was instrumental in helping find and deliver Willie."

"Duly noted. Thank you, Eli."

Eli bowed slightly in acknowledgement.

"General, is there any way I could get a vehicle from you? On my last visit I borrowed this one, and I would like to return it."

"*Borrowed* it, eh? From the lot?"

"Yes, sir."

"I think that is the least we can do." The general signaled a guard. "Son, have the motor pool send over one of those diesel dually Ford Super Duty cargoes we just got repaired."

"Yes, sir!"

He turned to the other guard. "Bring that passbook, son."

The guard brought a clipboard to the general, saluted and handed it to him. The general returned the salute, took a pen from his pocket, wrote on the paper on the clipboard, then signed it.

He tore the paper off and handed it to Frank. "Here you go, Mr. Lowman."

* * *Frank read the paper slowly, making sure he understood it. "Thanks, General. You ever get over my way, stop in for a drink. I make some mean pear cider."

"I would love to, Mr. Lowman. If we survive the next few weeks I just might do that."

The general stood at attention and saluted Frank, then turned and ordered the guards to take Willie and Clara to the infirmary. That no one unbound their arms or pulled the duct tape from their mouths made Willie apoplectic with rage, what little good it did him.

In a few minutes a green camo–painted Ford Super Duty diesel dually pulled up. A private got out with several forms that officially turned the vehicle over to one Frank Lowman for an indefinite time period. The private helped them move their gear, then took the keys for the truck they had driven up in and drove it away. Frank silently prayed that the owner, whoever it was, would see their truck again.

"What did he give you, Frank?" Eli asked as they drove away.

"A full pardon and a pass to get through the roadblocks," Frank said, smiling.

"We are going to look for Miss Max?"

"Next stop Mile Marker 2, State Route 9, Eli."

As happy as Frank was to have the heavy arm of the government off his shoulder, his worry over Max's safety was an ever-present weight on his soul.

* * *

Driving a military vehicle and using the pass provided by General Pratt, Frank and Eli made the trip back to Gaylesville in record time. Near where he'd had the run-in with the gang of road thugs, Frank pulled over.

"What is wrong, Mr. Frank?"

"This is where I pitted that four-wheeler. There may be salvage."

It didn't take long to find the wrecked four-wheeler—the buzzards dining on its former riders were hard to miss. A part of Frank felt remorse, seeing how young the bodies looked. He wondered if their parents knew or cared what had happened.

"This may be repairable; the engine is fine. Just handlebars, pedals and lights bent or broken," Eli said, dusting his clothes off. He noticed Frank staring at the bodies. "It is a sad thing, Mr. Frank, but they would not have hesitated to kill you and take everything you had."

"You are probably correct, Eli, but it just makes me sick. It took only three weeks to bring us from a relatively peaceful, civilized country to *Mad Max*."

Frank looked over at the remains. "Let's at least cover them up."

After piling on rocks to make a scavenger-proof shroud for the corpses, they lifted the wrecked four-wheeler into the truck and resumed their journey. It was two p.m. when they pulled into the Gaylesville roadblock.

"Frank! Good to see you. We were sure worried when them army guys hauled you off."

"Hi, Joe. Just a misunderstanding. Any problems?"

"Nope, real quiet. OK, come on through."

Joe signaled to the other men, who backed away two large pickups blocking the road.

Frank and Eli got on the homestretch.

George met them at the gate. Weeding and harvesting in the garden, he'd heard the diesel engine coming long before they got there.

"Frank, Eli! It is good to see you."

Frank opened the door on the large truck and climbed down from the driver's side. "George, it's good to be seen. Any problems?"

"Well, those army fellows came by and questioned me for a while, but since I really didn't know anything they really didn't bother me much." He smiled. "Especially when I broke out a few bottles of that perry you made."

"Wish we could stick around a while but we have to look for Max."

"You still haven't found her?" He leaned up to look in the truck, expecting to see Max in the backseat.

"No, but we found who kidnapped her. That rat Willie and his girlfriend."

"I hope you killed that rat bastard," George said with heat.

"No. Although Eli did get to wound him. We turned him over to the army at the Birmingham FEMA camp. That's where we got this nice ride." Frank patted the truck. "A brand new dually swapped for a low-life scum-truck. It was all worth it."

"We did learn where Max escaped from them," Eli said quietly.

"She never left Alabama," Frank added. "After we get something to eat I hope we can go get her."

Climbing into the dually, they all rode up to the collection of trailers and containers that made up the main BOL. George had leftover stew made from the lamb Eli cooked before all the mess began. He warmed it while Frank and Eli cleaned up.

"So Max escaped. I wish I coulda seen that," George said, passing bread across the table to Eli.

"Yep. She clocked Willie's girlfriend Clara with a tree branch and ran off into the woods around Mile Marker 2 on State Route 9."

Frank sopped up the spicy stew with a chunk of bread. Man, it was good.

"So she's been in the woods for nearly two days. She goin' to be OK out there?"

George looked horrified.

Frank laughed. "Max has been taking courses and practicing woodland survival for several years. I'll bet she could give lessons to a SEAR instructor."

He took a couple spoonfuls of stew and ate more bread. "George, has Martha radioed?"

George swallowed a bite, then said, "Nope. And I've been listening at the prescribed times. Not a peep."

"She was supposed to call in when her mom and the others got there. In the excitement I guess they forgot. I better radio them with the latest before we leave." He paused. "Right after some of that pear pie we had left. Unless you ate it all while we were gone, George!"

"I think there might be 'bout three pieces left. Let me go see . . ."

George disappeared into the main trailer.

"So that explains it," Eli said.

"Explains what?" Frank asked, pushing back from the table.

"Why you didn't seem too concerned about Max alone in the woods."

"Well, with Max it better be the woods that is afraid."

George returned with three pieces of pie.

Reynolds Farm

Outside Waleska, Georgia

Martha Reynolds was getting worried. Her mother, Katie, and her friends were supposed to arrive the previous day but they hadn't yet made it. She was about to call the Lowman BOL when the radio crackled from standby to live.

"Wayfarin' Stranger, this is Homefire. Out."

She rushed to the radio, recognizing her father's voice.

"Homefire, this is Wayfarin' Stranger. Over."

"Wayfarin', has Vagabond reached you? Over."

"Homefire, that is a no go. Repeat, that is a *no go*. Over."

"That is a no go as well, Wayfarin'. *Wood Nymph* has been kidnapped, repeat, Wood Nymph has been kidnapped, over."

Martha sat miserably on the chair by the radio table. Her mother and her friends and now her big sister—all missing. A tear streaked her cheek. Why couldn't people just leave them alone?

"Wayfarin', you there? Over."

She grabbed the mic. "Homefire, roger. Go get 'em, Dad," she said, a hitch in her voice.

"Roger, Pumkin. I intend to. Over."

Even through the radio, Martha heard how resolute her father was. She felt more confident. She knew once her father put his mind to something, it usually got done. She pushed the transmit button fiercely.

"Bring Vagabond and Wood Nymph home safe. Over."

"Roger that, honey. I will bring them as soon as I get them. Over and out."

"10-4 that. Over and out."

Putting down the mic, she put her hands together, closed her eyes and prayed to God for the safe return of her family members.

Her husband John found her still praying when he and the children came in from afternoon chores. He held her as she cried. Then she dried her eyes, straightened her spine and got to work.

If the entire family was likely to show up—and she felt confident they would—she had to get the place ready.

West Georgia Woods

Max stopped walking. The sweat was dripping down her forehead and stinging her eyes. Her blouse was sopping wet with sweat, her hair dank and greasy.

Looking up through the pine trees she could see the sun high in the sky—nearly noon. She pushed on through the woods, marginally cooler than in the full sun but just as humid. Not even a wisp of breeze broke the heat.

Stopping in a clearing, she used a fallen branch to brush pine straw and leaves from a circular patch for her afternoon fire. Her water bottle was empty so she pulled her water can from the sack that, she noticed, was getting tattered. The plastic bag, meant to last only a single trip from a store to someone's home, had done its new job admirably but was definitely worse for wear. She returned to the river to fill her water can.

Max descended the riverbank with great care. The last thing she needed was a turned or broken ankle. She noticed a large patch of blue fabric caught on a fallen tree in the water. Curious, she moved closer.

She recoiled when the current turned it over and revealed a fish- and crawdad-eaten face.

Steeling herself to the smell and grotesque state of the body, she untangled it and pulled it to the bank. He had been a good-looking boy until animals had ripped the waterlogged flesh from half his face. His backpack, though water-soaked, was still strapped on his small torso. With a silent prayer for this poor stranger, she removed the backpack and checked his pockets.

Other than lose change, soggy gum and a rusted pocketknife, there was nothing. Grimly, she scoured the bank for several yards in each direction, bringing all the stones she could to cover the poor child. She hoped she was not the only one to mourn him.

She lugged the still sodden backpack to her clearing. Setting her fire with the firesafe's morning coals, she laid out her food to warm, opened the backpack and removed the contents: one soaked copy of a *Hardy Boys* mystery book; a Gameboy that would never work again; a change of clothes; a full water bottle and a sodden mess that had once been a peanut-butter-and-jelly sandwich. No identification.

She wished she could have found at least his name, maybe eventually tell his family he had been found, mourned and buried.

While the backpack—and some socks she hoped would fit—dried by the fire, Max warmed the roast rabbit and artichokes. Using fine sand she cleaned the pocketknife of rust. It would be a much better tool than the one from her survival kit for cleaning fish, rabbits and whatever else. Using a flat rock, she honed the blade as sharp as possible while her dinner warmed.

When the food was ready Max gave a prayer of thanks and again prayed for the poor lost boy. The rabbit, though gamey, was great. Again she wished for a little salt, maybe some pepper, but the wild onions she'd found on the morning's hike had added a bit more flavor to both the rabbit and the jerusalem artichokes, which were starchy and fibrous but filling.

Between burying the boy and drying the backpack, it was too late for Max to resume her journey. The poacher's reel landed a few more trout, which she cleaned and staked out over the coals.

While the fish cooked, she reset the snare on another promising game trail.

By the time she set the snare, ate the trout and the little bit left of rabbit, and the artichokes, dusk was near. Unfolding the space blankets, she set up a nearly identical camp to that of the previous evening.

As the light faded and the whip-poor-wills and night animals started their chorus, Max fell asleep watching fireflies dance through the still night air.

It seemed like she had just nodded off when she was awakened by discomfort in her abdomen. Soon the pain was almost unbearable. She doubled over and passed an enormous amount of gas, which relieved the stomach pain even as it terrified small creatures for dozens of yards around.

Only then did she recall the alternate name for jerusalem artichokes: *fart*achokes.

She stood and walked—even checked the snare—which was empty.

Noting no further problems, she went back to sleep vowing to avoid the tasty but gas-inducing tubers.

Near Mile Marker 2

Alabama State Route 9

It was nearing dark when Frank called off the day's search.

"Well, we know *someone* camped here, and it appears to be Max's boot size."

He stood and brushed dirt from his hands.

"We could camp here," Eli offered, "and continue first light."

"We'll rest better back at the BOL. It's only a few miles. We'll load up a four-wheeler and try to catch up to her. She is one person on foot and we'll be two trying to find her trail. Maybe we can get ahead of her with the four-wheeler tomorrow."

"Perhaps one of us should go after Miss Katie and the others."

Frank was sick with worry over all of them, Katie *and* Max *and* the others. It was difficult to decide.

"Katie and Marlene have Earl and David," Frank said at last. "But Max has no one. Let's continue to search for Max."

They hiked back to their vehicle. Frank was always afraid to leave an unguarded vehicle. In this present reality, people would steal a working vehicle in a heartbeat. The military-style truck had a locking gas cap and they'd disabled the motor by pulling the main fuses. It should deter most thieves who'd been real estate salesmen only a few weeks ago.

After checking the truck for damage and vandalism, they restored the fuses and the diesel fired up, no problem. Frank drove and Eli had shotgun.

"Eli, get out the topo map and, assuming she'd stay near rivers or creeks, let's figure out her best course to her sister's place in Waleska."

"Good idea. If we can get ahead and move toward her we should find her quicker."

"Assuming she is stopping each night and not pushing a killing pace. In that terrain, let's assume she is making about ten miles a day."

While Eli applied his map skills to the problem, Frank drove in silence.

Camp

People's Militia of Rome

Katie and Marlene returned to the women's tent after chow. Everyone congratulated them on adding to the meals. The women's tent was hot and humid; the surrounding tents blocked what little breeze stirred the hot Georgia air. The only saving graces were the few battery-powered fans circulating stale air and camp smells; within minutes both Katie and Marlene were dizzy and nauseous. They lay on top of their sheets in as little clothing as they dared.
    "Katie, I've just got to know," Marlene whispered.
    "What, Marlene?" Katie tried not to sound exasperated but she'd been nearly asleep in spite of the heat, humidity and smells. Now it would take a half hour to get to that stage again.
    "How is hunting mushrooms going to get us out of here?"
    "I am building their trust. When the time is right we'll make our move. Did you find out if they are letting Earl see David?"
    "Yes, but only for a short time each day."
    "Good. How soon will David be out of the infirmary?"
    "At least two more days. According to the doctor the wound got infected."
    Good, thought Katie. *Should be just long enough.*
    "Where are they keeping Earl?"
    "In the single men's tent. Other side of the infirmary."
    "OK. Just be patient, Marlene. Trust me."

Now that Katie had a definite date to shoot for, she needed to move her plan up a day or so. She hoped she'd established enough trust to be able to betray.

* * *

Katie had woken several times during the night from the general discomfort of the camp. She was now feeling sweaty, uncomfortable and out of sorts with the world. In spite of her feelings she put on a happy face and joined Marlene at the simple toilette. The water was tepid but still felt good, washing off the night's sweat.

At the kitchen tent the morning was a repeat, with Katie and Marlene being sent out to forage for mushrooms.

"Katie, is this correct?"

Marlene held out a mushroom that looked almost identical to the chanterelles they were picking but was more orange.

"No. But remember where you got it."

Katie tucked the location away in her mind as Marlene pointed to an orange-looking cluster.

"Can we go further that way?" Katie asked their accompanying guard.

"Will it mean enough mushrooms for the men this time?" he asked with a smile.

Katie felt she could almost like the affable young man if he wasn't one of their captors.

"Yes, there should be many more in the shade of the ruined factory."

"Very well. Need help?" He offered to carry her canvas collection bag.

"No, thanks. I have it. But thank you for offering. Marlene, come on. Let's head over to the shade."

Marlene joined them; they walked about a hundred yards to the shaded areas near the ruined factory. In leaf mulch under oak trees they found large numbers of chanterelles as well as edible bi-color boletes.

"OK, we've filled our bags. I guess it's time to head back to the kitchen tent."

Katie didn't really want to leave the shade. A gentle, pleasant breeze had started.

"Do we have to? It is so nice here," Marlene said, echoing her thoughts.

"Yes. We wouldn't want Cooky to send us to the hospitality tents."

"He wouldn't!" their guard chipped in. "I mean, not for this."

Katie made a decision. "Let's pick those new ones as well. If we wait another day they may be overripe and ruined."

They detoured to the previous picking spot and gathered about half a bag of the orange mushrooms. The sun blazed and even the breeze didn't cool them much as they crossed the open area. By the time they reached the kitchen tent they were all sweating.

Katie once again offered to demonstrate to Cooky the edibility of the new ones, explaining they were a different type of chanterelle that went from gold to orange as they matured, and how it was getting late in the season and soon all the golden ones would turn orange. She threw in a bunch of jargon—fruiting bodies, spore patterns, gill structures—and soon Cooky's eyes glazed over. He waved her off and went to yell at another woman who had dropped meat on the dirt floor.

Under Katie's supervision, she and Marlene made sure no "mature" chanterelles made it into the women's stew.

"Marlene, tell David to tell Earl not to eat tonight and be ready to meet us at the gate."

"How? What about all the guards?"

"Let's just say they will be preoccupied."

* * *

About an hour after dinner and the guards had rotated through for chow, it started.

The lines at the latrines were soon long and full of cursing, doubled-over men. The smell of vomit and feces commingled; many hadn't made it to a toilet.

At the women's tent, Katie stood up.

"OK, girls," she called out. "All the men will be preoccupied for an hour or two. If you want out I suggest you get moving."

Just then Cooky ran past the women's tent clutching his stomach. If looks could kill, Marlene and Katie would be dead.

"That's our sign. Come on, Marlene."

Katie and Marlene grabbed what few items they had been allowed to keep and ran for the gates. The men were in various states of discomfort, from doubled over and sweating to laying in fetal position in their own waste on the ground. Katie and Marlene relieved a couple of them of their weapons as they feebly resisted. What few hadn't eaten or weren't yet affected were trying to figure out what happened and helping their companions.

At the gates Katie and Marlene rendezvoused with Earl and David, who each clutched a pistol and a rifle. In the parking lot across the street they found their Land Rover. Unfortunately, their supplies and weapons were gone, as were the keys. Earl pulled out the ignition wires and hot wired it; luckily it was an older-model Land Rover and didn't have a steering wheel lock.

"Wow, Katie." Earl was full of admiration. "What the heck did you do?".

"Come on, Katie, give it up." David was equally impressed. "That was incredible."

"Concentrate on driving," Katie answered. "The effects last only an hour or two."

"OK. But how did you do it," Earl insisted, as he raced out of town on Church Street.

"It was the orange mushrooms." Marlene looked to Katie for confirmation.

Katie explained, "Their common name is jack-o-lantern because of the orange color. I once long ago found what I thought was a huge chanterelle, just a little brighter color. I sautéed it in butter and ate it with garlic and salt. In about an hour I was seeing my shoes in the toilet. After that, I made sure I could identify it."

"Will it kill them," David asked. "They did take good care of me."

"No. It makes them *wish* they were dead. And maybe teach 'em a lesson about taking people against their will. Like I said, they should all be fine in an hour or two."

"Hopefully," Earl said, "we'll be safely at Martha's by then."

The trip took about forty minutes. The climb up the switchback driveway was the longest ride Katie could remember. When the two-story wood-frame house appeared she nearly cried. "Earl, give two long and one short toot of the horn. That's the signal we aren't robbers."

Martha, John and their five kids ages ten to a year and a half piled out of the door and across the wrap-around porch almost before the last horn toot. Katie threw open her door and jumped out, only to be surrounded by hugging, crying grandchildren.

"Where have you been, Mom? We were worried sick. So is Dad."

Martha grabbed her Mom in a fierce, tearful hug.

"I'd avoid Rome if I were you," Katie said. "Some redneck militia has it under control. They stopped us. *And* tried to forcefully recruit us."

"They tried to get me to join a couple months ago," John said, looking serious. "I went to one meeting and didn't like what I saw—anarchist rednecks and mall ninjas. How'd you escape?"

"Let's just say that knowing a chanterelle from a jack-o-lantern made all the difference," Katie said cryptically, as the rest of her crew laughed. "Seriously though, a few stray women may be asking for help; they escaped with us."

"We'll help all we can," John said. "Come on inside. We have the attic fan going and it's nice and cool."

"Glad you didn't join, John," Katie said. "They seem to believe might makes right. It's a dark path they're starting down."

Katie looked back at Marlene, Earl and David, standing at the car. "Martha, you remember Marlene, our neighbor. This is her husband, Earl, and their son, David."

"Glad to meet you all," Martha said. "Have you had supper?"

Martha looked concerned when they all started laughing again.

* * *

George was waiting for Frank and Eli at the gate to the BOL.

"Oh, no!" Frank exclaimed as they pulled up. "Must be more bad news. Why else would George suffer that thigh wound to get down to the gate?"

Frank rolled down the big truck's window.

"Frank, Katie and the crew are safely at Martha's!" George called out as soon as the window was down.

Frank felt an immense weight lifted. Now if they could just find Max they could all get back to rebuilding their lives.

Presidential Chambers

Birmingham FEMA Center

"This is outrageous!" President Wright screamed. "I want Frank Lowman and his band of cut-throats arrested *immediately!*"

But General Pratt had had enough. "Sir, with all due respect, your son is a psychotic son-of-a-bitch who deserved far worse than a shattered wrist."

"That will be *enough*, General. You are relieved of command."

The veins bulged on the president's head. "Better yet, put yourself under arrest for treason. You are a disgrace to your uniform."

"Well, sir, the apple didn't fall far from the tree," the general said, pressing a button on the portable transceiver in his pocket. At once, two heavily armed MPs stepped into the office.

"Sir, in accordance with the Twenty-fifth Amendment of the Constitution of the United States, I remove you from office until such time as you are adjudged fit to resume your duties."

Shots shattered the deadly silence as the president's Secret Service agents burst into the room and General Pratt's MPs fell dead.

"You think, General, that you're the only one with a secret button?" President Wright said with deadly earnest.

"Arrest the general for treason."

Reverend Sanders Goes Shopping

Reverend Sanders felt better than he had in many days. His infected scalp, now under control of antibiotics from the ransacked pharmacy, felt the best it had in days, and his vision was no longer doubling. Just how close he'd been to eternal rest, he really didn't want to know.

"I think it's time to head south, Reverend."

Nick seemed to delight in startling him. Nick's ability to appear from nowhere was unnerving; several times Sanders had almost shot him.

"I wish you'd stop that. One day, you'll get shot." Sanders took his hand from the snub-nosed .38 Bulldog tucked in his waistband.

"I *am* serious." Nick seemed earnest. "I think your leadership will be needed soon."

"OK. Let me pack the car," he said, while catching a whiff of eau-de-Reverend. He looked at his ruined suit. "First I need to wash up, and then get some new clothes."

"I believe we passed a retail zone with a Men's Wearhouse."

Nick, always helpful.

"And I'll bet the Bass Pro Shop has white gas. We can use it in the car."

After packing their meager supplies, they drove to the strip mall, which looked unhelpful: several stores showed signs of fire. The cell phone store was a complete burnout, as was the electronics superstore that was the mall anchor. Sanders wondered if the EMP had anything to do with what burned, or was it just anger from the crowd that their toys no longer worked.

The men's suit shop appeared relatively untouched other than smashed windows.

"Guess there isn't much call for suits these days," Nick smirked.

"Well—" Sanders parked in front of the men's store— "I'll check out the men's store. Think we can find something to clean me up?"

"The men's store may have wet wipes. Didn't they have to use them between customers?"

"OK, thanks. I'll check it out."

Sanders got out of the car. When he turned for his companion, Nick was nowhere to be seen.

It was dim inside the store after the bright sunshine outside. As his eyes adjusted to the dark interior, he saw that the store was in relatively good condition. He put a box of wet wipes to good use. He was then delighted to find a black suit that fit, and several dress shirts, socks, shoes and even high-end underwear. He tied his tie and from a display picked a semi-formal hard felt hat to cover his wound. After cleaning and rebandaging his wounded scalp, he donned his new clothes.

Admiring the new Reverend Sanders in a mirror, he started as Nick spoke up beside him.

"Looking good, Reverend! A man to be listened to."

"Where the *blazes* did *you* go?" Sanders said, adjusting his tie. He grabbed the sack with his new sets of clothes and the wet wipes, and headed for the car.

"At the sporting goods store. Found a couple gallons of white gas."

"I don't suppose you carried them to the car?"

"Bad back." Nick smiled. "You'd have to carry me if I tried."

I already am, Sanders thought to himself.

At the car, Sanders cleaned the driver's seat and steering wheel where his wounds had leaked various fluids over the last few days. He loaded his new duds in the backseat and went to the sporting goods store to retrieve the fuel.

The sporting goods store had faired far worse than the men's store. Goods were scattered everywhere, and most racks upended. Sanders found a decent sleeping bag and other camping items that had been overlooked, and three two-gallon cans of white gas for camping stoves. Six gallons would get him to Birmingham.

The gun counter, picked clean as it was, still yielded two fifty-round boxes of .38 Special ammo that would fit his wheel gun, and a couple .38 speedloaders, which he loaded and dropped in his suit-coat pocket. He found an inside-the-waistband holster that fit the revolver and took the time to conceal the gun. He guessed .38 Special wasn't a favored round anymore.

Sanders studied the scavenged pile and decided it was smarter to drive the car to the store. But as he stepped out, a Hispanic voice stopped him short.

"Hey, gringo, what are you doing, stealing from my turf?"

Blinded by the bright sunlight, Sanders held up his hand to block the glare. "Oh, just getting some supplies, young man."

"Nice suit, gringo. Not very practical, but nice."

Sanders could see the short, dark Hispanic standing a few feet away, casually aiming a large-caliber automatic at him. "Look, I don't want trouble. I am a man of God."

"A preacher, eh? Well, how about a contribution for the poor, preacher?" He smiled, revealing several gold teeth.

As Reverend Sanders' eyes continued to adjust, he could make out several tattoos on the man's face, obviously gang- or prison-related.

"Certainly, certainly. Let's go over to my car." The Reverend smiled and pointed. "Anything I have, you can take."

"Muchas gracias."

Sanders realized he had no choice as long as the man had the upper hand. He led the way to the parked car. His captor signaled with his gun that Sanders should stand aside while he looked in the backseat.

As he took his eyes off Sanders, the Reverend drew his revolver and emptied it into the Hispanic until the hammer clicked on an expended round.

"Nice shooting!"

Startled, Sanders turned and pulled the trigger, clicking again on an expended cartridge. "Damn it, Nick! *Stop* sneaking up on me."

"Language, Reverend, language. What would your congregation say?"

"Nothing. They're all dead."

Sanders opened the revolver's cylinder and, using the push rod, emptied the expended rounds, which tinkled merrily against the ground. Taking a speedloader from his pocket he loaded, closed and holstered the revolver. Nick gestured at the dead man spilling blood around the car's back tire. "His friends may be around. We'd better load up and skedaddle."

After driving to the sporting goods store, Sanders loaded the loot and poured the white gas into the tank, wishing for a funnel as he spilled while he poured. Luckily, none splashed on his new clothes. He used a wet wipe to remove the gas smell from his hands.

Without a backward glance Reverend Sanders and Nick drove out of town, heading south.

Along Georgia State Route 100

Near Coosa, Georgia

Frank and Eli set out early the next morning. Parking the truck near the coordinates where they figured Max would cross the road, they began backtracking through the woods. With the blackberry thickets, thorny vines and general chaos of southern second-growth timber, the four-wheeler was useless; they soon abandoned it and went on foot. The going was slow.

Frank thought back to when he was a child. A friend of the family—a half Aleutian Islander, half Dutchman named Leonard Stutsman—had stayed with them and worked as a rodman for a surveying company. Leonard had cursed the Southern Piedmont brambles. Frank now knew exactly what Leonard had experienced. Frank hoped Max wasn't fighting her way through with no gear to speak of.

"I hope we find her, Mr. Frank," Eli said as he slashed at brambles with a machete.

Frank had given up trying to get Eli to call him Frank. "We will, Eli. Have faith."

"Inshallah, Mr. Frank. Inshallah."

* * *

The day proved another typical southeastern summer day—hot and humid.

Max striped down as much as she dared. Too much skin, she risked getting eaten alive by mosquitos and deer flies, and burned by the sun; too little and she sweltered, risking dehydration from perspiration alone.

She followed a well-established game trail that fortuitously led in the direction she wanted to go. She couldn't help but notice the many odd tracks; they weren't deer, or rabbit, or anything else she'd known on the BOL property. They were nevertheless vaguely familiar, and she wracked her brain to recall where she'd seen them.

Coming up on a blackberry thicket, she heard a rustle, a squeal, and a deep snort that jolted the memory into her active mind—feral hogs!

She was just starting to sprint when a large, black, Russian boar broke cover. An oak tree with low branches offered a path out of harm's way as the boar charged beneath. She silently thanked all that garden hoeing and wood-splitting for improving her upper body strength.

Unfortunately, the boar was not alone. Soon several wild hogs were snorting and digging beneath the tree, looking for acorns and no doubt hoping she'd tumble out so the real feast could begin.

Great. How the hell do I get out of this?

She wished she had her AR-15, or better yet an AR-10 in the heavier .308 caliber. Even the clunky old Mosin–Nagant. Of course, she might as well wish for a squad of marines.

She settled in for what could be a long wait.

Max had nearly drifted off to sleep when the crack of a rifle jolted her upright. She scrambled for a hold, nearly falling from the oak. Several more shots rang out, scattering the hogs and leaving several—the large boar included—twitching in death beneath the tree.

"You can come down now!" a male voice called from the tree line.

"Show yourself first!" she shouted, scanning the tree line.

A figure dressed in a ghillie suit walked out of the tree line from where the shots came. The figure leaned a scoped rifle against a tree and, reaching up, removed the ghillie suit hood. Underneath was a red-headed, freckle-faced man with an infectious smile.

"OK, your turn! Come on down."

Max climbed down from her perch, dropping lightly to the ground. She was embarrassed with her mud-caked, sweaty appearance and stringy, greasy hair.

"Nice shooting. I don't know what I'd have done if you hadn't come along."

"These hogs have been tearing up my garden for a while. With things the way they are, it was get rid of 'em or starve. My name's Chet. Chet Rogers."

He smiled and extended his hand. "Nice, using mud for bugs. I'll have to try that now that DEET's not available."

"Max."

She wiped her hand on her pants and shook his. "Thanks for saving my butt."

"My pleasure. Look, we better get moving before they come back." He indicated the way she had wanted to go.

"Lead on. How far is Waleska?"

"Not far driving; another two days walking, maybe three." He paused. "Hold on. Let me take this suit off; I'm cooking in here."

He slithered out of the ghillie. Underneath he wore camo-style hunting pants and shirt, the shirt soaked with perspiration. And he had a backpack into which he stuffed the ghillie suit. He took two bottles of water from the pack and offered one to Max.

"Thanks. Been gettin' tired of river water."

She drank nearly the whole bottle; nothing had ever tasted so good.

"Whoa. You've been drinking *that?*" He pointed toward the river, barely visible through the undergrowth.

"Filtered and boiled best I could."

"How'd a nice girl like you get into a place like this," he said with a smile.

"Long story."

"Well, we have a long hike. My place is about two miles closer to Waleska." Chet said, shouldering his rifle.

* * *

As Frank and Eli reached a game trail, they heard a single shot in the distance, followed rapidly by several more, all from the same rifle, judging by sound and location.

"Come on, Eli, let's see who's shooting at what." He worried it had to do with Max.

They raced in the direction of the shots.

Hurry and stealth are not good companions in a forest. They made quite a racket closing in on the probable location, where they found a clearing with an oak tree and several dead hogs.

"Well, that explains the shots." Frank wiped his brow with his handkerchief. The run through the woods had been tiring in Georgia summer heat.

"Let's rest and figure out what next." Frank sat in the shade of the oak.

"I will stay over here, Mr. Frank."

Eli shunned the blood splatter and dead hogs.

"Oh, sorry, Eli. I forgot."

Frank pushed himself up and rejoined Eli at the clearing's edge. He checked that no blood had gotten on his clothes.

Eli, being Muslim, considered hogs unclean. Touching hogs made anyone unclean until ritually cleansed of the taint. Luckily, Frank hadn't inadvertently sat in any blood.

"Let's follow that game trail and maybe find the shooter," Frank said. "It heads in the direction Max would've gone."

Frank put away the compass he'd consulted.

* * *

A few hundred yards ahead, Max and Chet heard something following them.

"Damn. I'll bet that's those hogs. Let's take cover in that rhododendron patch. Maybe I can shoot a couple more."

Chet led Max to the thicket and, draping the ghillie suit across twisted trunks, made a suitable blind from which to snipe at the presumed hogs.

As the sounds approached, Chet raised his rifle and sighted along their back trail—

Max knocked his rifle up as Frank and Eli appeared.

"Ouch!" Chet said. The scope had nearly blacked his eye. "Damn, girl. I wasn't going to shoot *them*; they aren't hogs."

Chet was amazed as Max ran and hugged the strangers.

"Daddy! Thank God! Eli!" She hugged them both, obviously embarrassing Eli.

Chet stood off to side watching the reunion, but Max quickly pulled him over.

"This is Chet. He saved me from the hogs."

Chet was now the embarrassed one.

"Well, son, thanks. I'm glad you were here."

Frank shook Chet's hand.

"I was huntin' those pigs when I saw Max was treed. Did what anyone would've."

"Well, I don't know about that, son. These days chivalry seems to be getting rare."

"My cabin is about a mile and a half that way—" Chet pointed up the game trail.

"We have a truck back by the road." Frank consulted the compass. "About two hundred yards. Want a lift?"

As they hiked to the truck and then drove to Chet's cabin, Max told about her two days surviving in the woods.

"Smacked her good, eh?" Frank asked as they pulled into Chet's dirt driveway.

"Yep. Then took off like a rabbit. I figured Willie'd look after her while I escaped."

She looked smug.

"When we caught up to them, her bell was still rung pretty good."

"You *caught* them?" Max was clearly excited. "I hope you killed them!"

Frank was briefly taken aback by her vehemence. "No. I returned 'em to Willie's father."

"You know his *father?*" Now Max was floored.

"Yup. President Wright."

She was speechless.

"That does it," Chet said. "You aren't allowed to leave until you tell me the full story."

Rome and Waleska

At the headquarters of the Peoples Militia of Rome, the Brigadier was pissed. He gazed out at his most trusted men, the ones who'd been part of the militia from the start, only a few weeks ago when they met in his basement and fantasized about the end of the world.

"Well, that bitch got in the first blow."

The men, still piqued and pale from the severe runs and heaves brought on by Katie's jack-o-lantern mushrooms, muttered angrily in agreement.

"I have men tracking them. As soon as they call in we will take our revenge!"

The men cheered. They all felt foolish at being bested by one woman and a pound of fungus. Cooky was especially angry, having placed his trust in Katie only to be betrayed.

A scout roared up on an off-road motorcycle, stopping in a cloud of dust.

"We found them, sir. On a farm over in Waleska."

* * *

Sergeant Andrews led his two Humvees toward Waleska.

According to information they squeezed out of IRS records and other sources, Frank Lowman's youngest daughter, Martha, and her husband, John Reynolds, had a farm outside of this small town. His orders—arrest Frank Lowman and his entire family—didn't sit well with him.

Arresting Lowman seemed on the up-and-up. Barracks gossip said he'd just about destroyed the president's son's right wrist, and perpetrated other crimes against the boy. Other scuttlebutt said the little prick deserved it. But arresting Lowman's whole family went against the grain, even when he had to follow orders.

As the two-vehicle convoy reached the drive leading to the Reynolds Farm, he called a halt and brought his men together.

"Alright. You men in Vehicle 2 will deploy into that bunch of trees and await orders. I will take Vehicle 1 up and secure the main house."

"Sir, are we authorized to shoot?"

"Only if fired upon. As far as we know these people are noncombatants."

"Then why are we arresting them?"

Andrews looked sharply at the questioner. "Because those are our orders. Any *questions?*" His tone said there better not be. "Private Winston, because you are our sole female, as soon as we secure the adults, I want you to take the children."

"Sarge," Winston scowled, "I hate children."

"They'll trust *you* more than any of *these* craggy sons of bitches."

He gestured at the rest of the men, who laughed.

"Yes, sir."

"Don't call me *sir*. I *work* for a living."

"Yes, Sergeant."

Vehicle 1 watched as Vehicle 2 made its way up the drive and into the woods. Once Andrews was satisfied they were concealed, he drove toward the house.

* * *

Inside the house, John swore he heard a vehicle. "Hey, you guys hear *that?*"

"Yes, I hear it too. Better grab the guns."

Earl headed to the gun safe, but had to wait until John could enter the combination.

Just as John began entering the code, the door burst open and two Rangers rushed in with weapons at the ready. The children screamed and cried.

"We're unarmed!" John called out, tossing his side arm to the floor; Earl did likewise.

"Lay down on the floor, *now!*" a Ranger screamed at them, rushing to the guns and kicking them aside.

Everyone was on the floor, the children crying, when Sergeant Andrews entered with the rest of his men.

"At ease, men. I think you have them," he said dryly as he holstered his side arm. "Private Winston, take the children into one of the bedrooms."

PFC Winston, standing beside him, safetied her weapon and slung it, then signaled that the children should stand and follow her.

With a fearful glance at Martha, who tried to look reassuring, the children followed PFC Winston out of the room. At a signal from Andrews, his men quickly applied tie-cuffs to the prone adults, then helped them to their feet and into chairs.

Grabbing a spindle-back chair, Sergeant Andrews turned it around, sat, leaned forward over the back, and glared straight at them, a glare rumored to peel paint off a barrack's walls.

"Alright," he growled, "where is Frank Lowman?"

Presidential Chambers

Birmingham FEMA Camp

Secretary of State Daily was terrified. Several bearers of bad news had been arrested. He'd heard that General Pratt was to be executed for treason. He waited nervously to make his briefing.

"You can go in now, Mr. Secretary."

Daily could tell by Cathy's tone that she empathized with his plight.

He tried not to stare at the rug stains. There hadn't been time to replace it and cleaners hadn't removed all the blood.

"Secretary Daily!" The president smiled but his eyes were hard. "Please, sit."

"Yes, sir."

Daily sat and opened his briefing notes.

"Care for water?"

President Wright stood and held up a pitcher. Daily had heard the president was most dangerous when he was being nice.

"No thank you, sir. I had some before I came in."

"Well then, let's get down to it. *Tempus Fugit.*"

He set the pitcher on a silver tray and sat joylessly in his overstuffed office chair.

Daily tried to get comfortable on the hard wooden chair. He cleared his throat and began. "I'm afraid it doesn't look good, sir."

The president's eyes narrowed even as he kept smiling.

"All the major California cities," Daily said, "have a Chinese contingent. Their navy has all but blockaded San Francisco, San Diego and as far north as Seattle. They are advancing inland with their supposed 'aid,' distributed by armed troops. They leave a garrison in each town."

The secretary audibly gulped, feeling as if he was reading his own execution order.

"Mexico—with aid from several countries in Central and South America and from Cuba—has taken territory in Texas under the color of 'pacification of lawlessness,' in a line from Midland to Corpus Christi. The Texas National Guard has held that line but they are running out of ammo and desertion rates are high."

Daily risked a glance at the president. He did not like what he saw.

"Canada is holding our northern areas secure from Russian incursion, but we have had no word out of Alaska for two days. All missions sent there have failed to respond after crossing into Russian-held territory."

He closed the folder.

The veins on President Wright's forehead were distended and his color was rising, even though he still smiled. "Keep me posted. Have General Bromley come in."

Secretary Daily nearly knocked the chair over as he hastened out.

* * *

"He wants General Bromley next," Daily said to Cathy, wiping his brow with a dingy white handkerchief.

Wright had promoted Bromley after the arrest of General Pratt and placed him in charge of the Birmingham military units. He also tasked him with apprehending and detaining Frank Lowman and his family. But today he had a different mission for his new general.

"General! Please, sit."

"Yes, sir." Bromley sat, appearing to be attentive.

"What have you heard about Project Shiva?"

The president's cold eyes bored into Bromley's, who felt a cold sweat breaking out on his forehead.

"Just rumors, sir."

"Please, tell these rumors to me."

"Mythic Star Wars stuff, sir. Secret satellites, kinetic warheads, clandestine Shuttle missions, that kind of thing. Killer satellites in stationary orbit above all major countries, capable of destroying much of that country's infrastructure without nukes. Stuff in blatant violation of peaceful-use-of-space treaties."

"What if I told you it *wasn't* mythic?"

The president sat back and studied Bromley. "That those satellites exist."

"I would have to take your word for it, sir. I don't have clearance for that level of information."

"You do now."

The president tossed the Shiva folder across the desk.

It landed with a dull thud of finality.

Reynolds Farm

Frank fidgeted nervously as he drove the last bit of driveway up to Martha's house. Finally, his entire family was together again. As he cleared the tree line surrounding the central acre of Martha and John's property, where their house was located, he slammed on the brakes, nearly sending Eli and Max into the dash of the truck. Parked in front of the house was a military Humvee, and two Rangers stood guard with AR-16s at the ready.

"Damn, Damn, *Damn!*" Frank pounded the steering wheel. "I should've known it was too good to be true."

He slammed the big truck into reverse to haul down the driveway to a turnaround, but when he looked in the rearview mirror he slammed on the brakes again. A second Humvee had them blocked. The only way open was forward.

"Frank Lowman—drop your weapons out the windows." The speaker on top of the Humvee blared out the command. *"Then proceed forward."*

With Rangers with AR-4 and AR-16 rifles covering them from both behind and front, Frank, Eli and Max had no choice but to comply. They dropped the .40-cal automatics and AR-15s out the car window and then slowly pulled up next to the other Humvee.

"Turn off the vehicle. Then exit, showing your hands."

The three had a sinking feeling. A couple Rangers walked under cover from the Humvee and, after tie-cuffing their hands behind their backs, marched them to the house, up the steps and inside.

* * *

What Frank saw inside angered him more—his entire family was cuffed. He didn't see his grandchildren but he assumed they were detained in a bedroom, probably under armed guard.

"What the hell is going on here, Sergeant?"

Frank bit off the words, seething with rage at the treatment of his innocent family. "I have a pardon from General Pratt."

"Sir, General Pratt has been arrested for treason. My orders are to arrest you *and* your family, and bring you *all* to Birmingham." The sergeant was grim-faced. "Charges are sedition, and attacking and wounding the president's son."

"Mr. Frank is innocent. I am the one who shot him," Eli confessed. "Mr. Willie had a gun to Mr. Frank's head and was preparing to murder him. I had no choice."

"You know, I don't care. My orders are to bring you all in. Once you get to Birmingham, the courts can decide who is guilty."

"Leave my family out of this. Take Eli and me, but leave them be."

"My orders are the *entire* family."

"But—"

Frank's retort was cut off by the sound of gunfire.

"Miller, Johnston, you stay here with Winston and guard the Lowmans. The rest come with me. Miller, you're in charge." The sergeant drew his service weapon and headed out the front door followed by the other Rangers.

A shot smashed a window.

"Everyone down!" Frank called out as he dropped to the floor, his tie-cuffed hands making such a move extremely awkward.

With a curse, he applied a trick he'd seen on the internet about how to break tie-wrap cuffs by bringing them around in front then slamming them down across the hips as hard as possible. He cursed being old, as it was nearly impossible to get his cuffed wrists down past his legs and over his boots, but he eventually succeeded. Sharp pains in his back told him he'd pay for it later but now, high on adrenalin, he barely noticed it.

Amazingly, the trick worked.

More shots pierced the windows and splintered into walls and furniture. Frank wiggled to a window and snuck a quick glance, pulling his head down as more shots shattered what was left of the glass.

"A bunch of yahoos in camo!" he called out.

More shots pinged off the stack-stone exterior, the only thing keeping bullets from peppering the inside.

"Damn. It must be the militia," Katie said, staying low to the floor.

"Who?" Corporal Miller asked, as he charged his weapon and prepared to fire back.

"A bunch of crazies who call themselves the People's Militia of Rome. They took four of us captive but we escaped." Katie yelled over the gunfire. "Probably pissed them off. Looks like they tracked us down."

Corporal Miller and Specialist Johnston eyed each other, nodded in unison and then popped up into the window and ripped off a couple of automatic bursts as suppression fire. Then the corporal looked out the window to get an idea of what they were up against—only to catch a round in the forehead, dropping him instantly, dead.

"We are sitting ducks, Johnston," Frank shouted at the remaining Ranger. "We need weapons and a plan to get out of here."

Just then the noise level ratcheted up as someone cut loose with a SAW, an M249 squad assault weapon. Hopefully it was the Rangers or they were royally screwed. Johnston realized that Frank was right. He allowed Frank to cut loose the other family members and arm themselves from John's gun safe.

Johnston called out to PFC Winston that Martha and another female was coming, as Martha and Max crawled the hall to check on the children, Martha clutching a 12-gage Maverick shotgun holding seven rounds in its tubular magazine. Frank grabbed a .30-06 Remington 742 with a five-round magazine and Eli a goose gun. John grabbed an AR-15 and Earl and David had a mix of automatic and wheel guns.

"There's an escape tunnel in the basement," John suggested. "We can get the kids and women out, and then flank them."

Specialist Johnston thought a moment then nodded affirmative.

Katie, Max and Marlene helped Martha herd the children downstairs first, then the men followed. The chaotic clatters and booms of a firefight followed them into the cool, dark basement. John flipped on a switch and led them to a large pantry, revealing shelf after shelf of freeze-dried and canned goods. He then ran to a back wall were he tripped a hidden latch on a canned-asparagus shelf. The pantry swung away, revealing a six-foot-diameter "storm" drain leading away from the house.

"Hurry!" John gestured to the women and children.

With Max in the lead with another Maverick shotgun and the children close behind, they all hurried down the tunnel. At the end, they waited until Specialist Johnston and PFC Winston caught up. "OK. Winston and I will go out first and make sure it's clear. Then you women and children get out and disperse into the woods. David, you stay here and guard the tunnel. You men—" Johnston gestured to Frank, Eli, John and Earl—"follow us."

John tripped the release. The tunnel's concealed outer opening, located in a copse of trees and boulders several dozen yards from the house, swung up. They were hidden from the main skirmish.

After a quick reconnaissance, Johnston signaled it was clear and the women and children ran into the woods.

"OK, John, talk to me," said Johnston.

"Yes, sir?"

"This is your property. What's the best way to get behind those assholes?"

They could hear the ripping of the SAW, the pop of AR-15s and the rattle of AK-47s, as well as the single bangs of shotgun, deer and other hunting guns.

"Well, there's a gully running behind their position," John said. "About twenty yards into the woods. If we stay low we should be able to get behind them unnoticed."

"OK, good. Winston and I will take lead. When we signal, you come up behind us and provide cover until we get into position."

Running low, they reached the gully and jumped into its shallow creek. Crouching, they followed it toward the chaos of battle. Going to meet an unknown number of assailants with unknown arms and capabilities was quite frankly scarring the crap out the Johnston, but he'd faced worse in the Middle East.

Johnston held up his hand and made a fist; everyone stopped. He peered over the rim of the gully then dropped back down. Keying his radio, he called Sergeant Andrews.

"Sarge, we're in a flanking position, awaiting orders."

"What the hell? I thought you were in the house!"

"We were, but the house has an escape tunnel. One friendly now at the end. We are now in a gully right behind the hostiles."

"No shit! Give me a landmark so we don't chop you with the SAW."

"That really tall pine, the one with the dead branch. We are east of it."

"Got it. We'll open up to give you cover. You come forward and as soon as we let up, cut those buttholes a new one."

"Roger."

Johnston signaled to Winston. Both switched out their partials for fresh magazines.

"OK. All hands," Johnston said, "get ready to provide cover. As soon as the SAW opens up, we start running."

Everyone nodded that they understood.

* * *

It seemed like forever even though it was actually only a few seconds.

When the SAW started ripping, shredding the landscape to the west of the large pine pointed out by Johnston, he signaled to Winston and they both clambered quickly out of the gully and crab-ran toward the battle. And Frank and the other civilians also opened up, careful to avoid hitting the two soldiers as they rushed the militia's flank.

Johnston saw several camo-ed figures crouched in the tree line shooting a hodge-podge of weapons at the farmhouse. He stopped, kneeled and aimed, using the red-dot sight on his AR-16 to pick off the militiamen one by one. Beside him, Winston was doing the same. Every few shots they moved to a new position.

Flanked and out-gunned, the militia was soon in full rout. It was over.

* * *

As the surviving militia members were rounded up, Frank entered the woods behind the house. "Martha . . . ! Katie . . . ! Max . . . ! It's all over. You can come out."

He heard the clicks of weapons being safetied and soon Martha, Katie, Max and his grandchildren surrounded him. After a few tearful hugs they headed toward the house.

Evelyn, his youngest granddaughter, insisted he carry her, and clung fiercely to his neck. Isaiah, his youngest grandson, held his hand tightly as they walked across the backyard.

Katie entered the main room in the farmhouse and saw whom the Rangers had captured.

Before anyone could stop her, she launched herself at the tall figure she recognized as the Brigadier and knocked him to the ground, pummeling him with her fists and clawing at his eyes.

"You bastard! Opening fire on my grandchildren! I'm gonna kill you!"

It took two of Sergeant Andrews' men to pull her off the cuffed "brigadier."

* * *

After hearing Katie, Marlene, Earl and David's stories, Sergeant Andrews faced a dilemma.

On one hand, he had his orders to bring in the Lowmans. On the other hand, the People's Militia posed a clear and present danger to the city of Rome and surroundings.

Knowing it could cost him his rank, he made a decision.

"Look, everyone, I'm supposed to bring you in. But I'll be honest. Even with the SAW those yahoos had the drop on us. Without your help, it would've been much more difficult if not impossible to subdue them. So I'll tell you what. I'm going to call in a couple other patrols and we are going to take care of the remainder of this militia. But, I am going to be back for you. For now, I release you on your own recognizance. You can return to your Alabama farm or you can stay here, but it will go hard if you run."

"Sergeant," Frank looked Andrews in the eye, "Eli and I will be glad to go back with you. But if this still includes my whole family, you'd better take us now."

The sergeant pondered again, then said, "OK, fine. Only you and Eli. I don't know how long it will take to eliminate this militia, but when we finish, you better be ready for Birmingham."

"You leave my family out of it, Sergeant, and you have my word."

Frank held out his hand; the sergeant shook it firmly.

"Alright, soldiers, saddle up," Sergeant Andrews called. "We need to rendezvous with the other patrols and make a plan for this militia. Specialist Johnston, form up a squad and take these prisoners to Birmingham."

Sergeant Andrews saluted Frank and bowed to the women as his patrol headed out. "Don't worry about the mess outside, or Miller's body inside; my soldiers will handle it," he tossed back over his shoulder.

John, Frank's son-in-law, surveyed the wreckage of his house with dismay. "Damn it, Frank, you sure make one hell of an entrance."

"We'll help you clean up," Frank said, "Then we need to head back to the BOL."

Camp Birmingham FEMA Center

Reverend Sanders slowed the car as they neared the first checkpoint. When he turned to ask Nick for advice, Nick was nowhere to be found. The Reverend's moment of mental uncertainty was interrupted by the checkpoint officer:
"Please keep your hands where we can see them and step out of the vehicle."
Sanders discretely pulled the revolver, slid it between the seats, and then got out with his hands up. "I'm not armed."
One officer covered him with an AR-16 while the other searched him.
"Where is the gun that goes in this holster?"
"I removed it before getting out of the car." Sanders felt it would be wise to tell the truth. "It is between the seats."
"Do you have any ID?"
Sanders pulled his battered wallet from his new suit pocket and showed his driver's license.
"*Reverend* Sanders, is it? Please wait here. Do not move."
He took Sanders' ID and walked to the Humvee at the roadblock.
Sanders felt sweat start as the officer made a radio call. The tension was stretching unbearably when the officer finally exited the Humvee, walked over and handed him his driver's license.
"What's your business in Birmingham, Reverend?"

"I want to help at the camp." He tried his best congregation-pleasing smile. "I understand they need spiritual guidance."

"Very well, sir. Register with the gate when you get there." He gestured that Sanders was free to leave.

Sanders pulled away, wondering what the heck happened to Nick.

* * *

"Well now, looks like ol' Billy has got hisself hurt."

William opened his eyes. The medication prescribed for the pain from his wrist after the reconstructive surgery rendered him groggy and half alert. He tried to focus on the apparition beside the bed.

"Nick! How the hell did you get in here? Good to see you, buddy."

Jerking awake from a fitful doze in the bedside chair, Clara felt her hackles rise as she realized William was talking to Nick.

"That's unimportant. What *is* important—Reverend Sanders is on his way here."

"That asshole nearly got me killed."

William tried to sit but the various tubes, bandages and his medicated grogginess made it difficult. He collapsed onto the bed. Clutching for a bedpan, he retched into it, an aftereffect of the pain meds.

"Now, now. As I recall you joined him for a chance at Lowman. You got that chance. Of course, doesn't look like it ended up so well . . ."

"Rub it in, you prick, rub it in."

Putting the bedpan down but well within reach, William turned his face away from Nick and closed his eyes.

"Look, Bill, you need to get Sanders in good with your old man."

"Wha— Why?" William turned back to Nick, now more awake.

"I'll tell you later. If your dad asks, give Sanders an endorsement. Tell him how that Eli fellow killed Sanders' son and all the Reverend was trying to do was bring Eli in for justice."

"But—"

"No buts, Billy. Look, I have to go. Don't worry, I won't desert you."

Nick made to go but William was having none of it. "Where have *you been!* You left me. Now you come back, wanting shit."

Nick stopped a moment. "It's part of a plan. And you, Bill, are a big part of it. You are important. *You* of all people should know I'm difficult to get rid of once invited in." He looked up, as if he were listening. "Yep, time to head out. Remember what I said."

Nick moved to the door, as Bill's eyes grew heavy. Eyes closed, he missed Nick's exit.

The door opened and the doctor entered.

"So, how are we today, William," he asked in a chipper tone, picking up the chart. "You should thank whoever gave you first aid."

"What!"

"Whoever cleaned your wound, applied the quick clot and field bandages probably saved you *and* your hand. Without proper treatment, you might have bled out, or at the very least lost the use of your hand. Because it was immediately so well treated we were able to reattach it well enough that you should regain almost full use."

The doctor marked a few things on the chart.

"He also caused it," William muttered.

"I don't know what to say, Mr. Wright. Obviously he didn't want to kill you or he'd have let you alone, let you bleed out." He clipped the chart on the bed end. "If you need anything, push the button."

The doctor checked the morphine level in the infusion pump, waved to Clara and left.

In the chair, Clara sat dejected. *Damn it! Why did Nick have to come back now?*

* * *

General Bromley laid the folder in his lap when he finished.

Removing his reading glasses, he rubbed his tired eyes. "This is all well and good, sir, but the only Shiva initiators were on Air Force One and, far as I can tell," he held up the folder, "in the Oval Office."

"Exactly why I need you, Bromley. For a special mission. Your objective: return to DC and retrieve the Oval Office Shiva initiator."

"But sir, we don't know the status of the White House. It could be a smoking ruin."

"I'm having the intelligence wonks move a satellite into position so we can take a look. They should have data to me shortly."

"How will my men recognize it? Nothing in this file describes it. No diagrams . . . no pictures . . ."

"I assume it will resemble the nuclear codes briefcase. Hell, just have them bring back any and all electronic devices they find."

"Yes, sir."

"Assemble a team. Soon as I get more intelligence I'll send it over. I don't need to tell you this is eyes-only. Tell them *to bring back* the electronics, not what it is."

Bromley stood, handed the folder across the desk and saluted. Turning sharply, he left the president's office.

No sooner did the door close than the intercom buzzed. "Yes, Cathy?"

"Mr. President, the front gate called. A Reverend Sanders is out there. He says he knows your son; the guards want guidance."

President Wright was thoughtful, remembering what the files had said about this Reverend Sanders and the Lowmans. Of course, Sanders supposedly was dead, but anyone who hated Frank Lowman was a probable friend.

"Cathy, let Reverend Sanders in. See if he needs anything, then make him comfortable. I have to talk to my son."

"Yes, sir." The intercom clicked off.

Standing, Wright winced at a minor back cramp. He really should get more sleep. Maybe once this Lowman business was wrapped up he could. With his entourage of Naval attachés and Secret Service bodyguards, he walked across the compound to the hospital.

* * *

As President Wright strode into his son's room, Clara nearly tripped, rising up from the chair.

"No need to get up, Clara, please. May I call you *Clara?*"

The president smiled at her, which flustered her even more. Unsure what to do, she remained standing. The president sat gently on the edge of Bill's bed; the jostling made Bill wince.

"William, how are you today?"

"Fine, for having my hand half shot off."

"The doctor tells me you should get back nearly full use."

"Good. I'd hate to have to learn to jack off left-handed."

Bill turned away from his father.

"William, I know I haven't always been the best father—"

"Like, never," Bill said coldly.

President Wright gritted his teeth, then made an effort to relax. "Listen, I want to make up for it. Once we get the country back on track, I want to spend more time with you."

He reached to give a reassuring pat to Bill's shoulder, but Bill flinched and said, "What do you want? I'm trying to rest."

Wright pulled his hand as if he'd been burned. "A friend of yours is at the gate."

"Nick?" Bill turned hopefully to his father.

"No. A Reverend Sanders."

President Wright saw his son's face fall. Hardly the result to expect from good news.

"It seems he survived Lowman's attack."

Bill perked up at the odd phrasing. "Sanders was trying to get that Muslim Eli who killed his son. Trying to get him to Fort Payne so the sheriff could arrest him."

"That Lowman gang is getting rounded up even as we speak, son."

Bill brightened. The president felt relieved when his son smiled at him. "We'll have Frank Lowman before the end of the week."

"I would like that. I would like that a lot, Dad."

* * *

Reverend Sanders flinched with each trigger pull on the auto-suture staple gun in the doctor's hand. The doc used his other gloved hand to hold closed the edges of Sanders' scalp wound.

"If you hadn't taken good care of this it could've killed you."

Snick, snick, snick.

"You know something funny? We pay over a hundred dollars each for these single-use suture staple guns." He paused and held the Star Trek phaser–looking device up to the light. "My son-in-law bought the same thing from a veterinary supply house for ten bucks."

Snick, snick, snick.

"There. Should be good as new in about ten days. Come back and we'll remove the staples. Keep taking those antibiotics."

He tossed the gun into the medical waste bucket even though it still held most of its staples allotment. "Damn!" he cried, fishing it out and setting it on the tray. "Not the old world, anymore. We have to use things up. I hear they're trying to reload them."

He pulled off his gloves and stuffed them into the waste. "At least we don't have to reuse gloves, yet."

"How'd the x-rays turn out?"

Reverend Sanders' forehead felt tight and he imagined the two teeth on each of the twenty staples biting into his flesh. Of course, that was ridiculous with as much painkiller as the doctor injected prior to suturing.

"You are a lucky man, Reverend. God must be with you. I'm sure it rang your chimes for a couple days, but no permanent damage. Must have been low caliber. They can bounce off that hard part of the skull."

"I think it was a .38."

"Yep. Several cases in the literature of this very thing. Never seen it myself, though. Not til now. Here—" the doctor handed Sanders antibacterial ointment. "The nurse will give you gauze. Change the dressing every day and smear this along the edges. Should help reduce scarring."

As Sanders was getting his shirt and suit coat back on, someone knocked at the door.

"Come in?"

"Reverend Sanders! My son tells me good things about you."

President Wright, accompanied by his Secret Service guards, suddenly filled the small treatment room. "The doc taking good care of you?"

"Yes, sir. Thank you, Mr. President. Your boy was very helpful in my attempt to get justice."

In fact, Sanders didn't remember who the president's son was.

"Well, I have my men arresting Lowman and his mob even as we stand here."

"Eli?"

"Ah, Eli . . . ? Oh, Lowman's pet Muslim. Yes, him too."

President Wright held out his soft, manicured politician's hand. The Reverend dutifully shook it.

"So tell me, Reverend," the president said. "What brings you to us?"

"Frankly, Mr. President, I want to help. There seems to be plenty of lost sheep in search of a shepherd in the camps."

"That there are, Reverend, that there are. But I may have a more important job for you. Tell you what, you follow Agent Gault here over to the mess and get a good meal. And afterward, we'll talk."

Reynolds Farm

At Martha and John's the men made short work of cleaning up the major damage. They patched holes, boarded up the shot-out windows with plywood from John's barn, and replaced splintered porch rails. While not 100 percent, the house was soon livable again.

As the men worked outside, the women fixed a large supper and watched the children.

"Well, I think that's about all we can do today. I'll get over to town next week and beg, borrow or steal replacement glass."

John paused and, removing his dark-blue NRA ball cap, used an off-white handkerchief to wipe sweat from his forehead.

"If you men can take a break, dinner's almost ready." Martha called out the door. "Get in here and clean up!"

"Don't need to call us twice, daughter."

Frank was happy. Well, at least as happy as anyone could be in a post-apocalyptic world. After all, his family was finally safe, and they had shelter and food. While dark times may be ahead, dealing with President Wright and his psychotic son, he wasn't going to borrow trouble from the future.

They settled in at the large dining-room table and Frank said a prayer of thanks before eating. Ham, cornbread, pole beans, corn on the cob and mashed potatoes with red-eye gravy filled the air with sumptuous aromas and filled the table with a gorgeous view.

"Wish you all could stay a day or two," Martha said as she buttered corn for her youngest son and passed him the dripping ear. How he ate corn on the cob with several teeth missing was a mystery.

"I wish we could too, Pumpkin," Frank answered, spearing a slice of ham as it sailed past. "But we have to get back to the BOL before someone tries to take it out from under us."

He plopped a goodly serving of potatoes on his plate beside the ham and ladled gravy over it. "We also don't want to eat up all your supplies, since we didn't manage to bring any with us."

"We have plenty, Dad. Those three pigs we slaughtered gave us plenty of meat and the garden has been a real blessing this year."

She popped her eldest on the back of the head to stop him from teasing his little sister.

"Tough times coming. We all may need everything we have and then some."

Eli made a good meal of everything but the pork and gravy. Martha warmed leftover chicken for him.

"Inshallah, my friends." he said.

At the puzzled looks from Martha and the children, he explained, "It means *as God wills.*"

"Inshallah, then, to you, Eli. And thanks for pulling Dad's can from the fire."

"He pulled out all of us a couple of times."

Katie smiled at Eli, who looked embarrassed.

"You all took me in when no one else would. You risked your lives for me against Reverend Sanders. It is I who should be grateful." He looked down. "I am sorry to have caused such a wonderful family so much trouble."

"Eli, *Sanders* was trouble. *You* may have provoked him to show his true self early, but eventually he would have showed it on his own, and by then he could have had many more zealots, and it would have been much harder to stop him."

"From your tongue to Allah's ears, Miss Katie."

The remainder of the meal was spent planning the return to the BOL. John would loan weapons until they could get back home, then Eli would do a quick round-trip to return them.

It was a tearful good-bye after supper, as they got back into the vehicles—the classic Land Rover and the modern super truck seemingly incongruous together.

With Frank, Eli and Max in the lead truck and the rest in the Rover, they caravanned to the BOL with no surprises.

George was happy to see them as the pulled in after sunset.

Cafeteria

Birmingham FEMA Center

Reverend Sanders finished his second plate of food. Perhaps not up to five-star restaurant standards, it was nonetheless nourishing and filling, and better by far than what he'd been eating for the last two weeks.

Agent Gault had stood by while the Reverend ate. When he finished the last plate, Agent Gault used his wrist mic to inform the president's detail that he and the Reverend would be coming to the president's compound as instructed. With Gault in the lead, the Reverend followed, wondering what the president wanted with a failed, small-town preacher. He didn't have long to wait.

"Please sit, Reverend. Something to drink? Water? Maybe tea?"

The president gestured to a tray with pitchers of various beverages.

"No, sir. I am quite full from dinner."

Sanders sat on the hard wooden chair.

"Excellent. I'm glad they took good care of you." He circled the desk and sat in the overstuffed office chair. "You know, before the attack America was lost, adrift. We had no rudder."

Not knowing where this was leading, Sanders kept quiet.

"We had all sorts of perversions being accepted as normal, people destroying long-held beliefs, rewriting history. I want to put the country on a firm footing." He looked directly into Reverend Sanders' eyes. "I want you to help me."

"But Mr. President, separation of church and—"

"All that is gone now, Reverend. Shoot, it never said that in the Constitution anyway— just some dunderheaded Supreme Court mumbo-jumbo." He paused to sip some water. "I want you to help me rekindle *faith*. Bring back the firm beliefs this country was founded on. Will you do that, Reverend?"

"Sir, that is quite a large order. There is so much chaos."

"The way you stood up for justice against the heathens tells me you're the right man, Sanders. We have godless Commies, Maoists, Papists, Muslims—all attacking our borders. And, of course, we have the rot from within. Reverend, I *need* your help."

The Reverend swallowed, his throat suddenly dry. "I will try, sir."

"Good. Tell you what, take a couple of days. Rest up, heal, and then we'll sit and make plans." The president turned to face the window onto the camps.

"Agent Gault will show you to your quarters."

Stockade

Birmingham FEMA Center

General Pratt's first night in the stockade was not very comfortable. He tossed and turned, wondering if there would be a farce trial or a simple execution by President Wright's thugs. The room had one small window—barred, of course—but it let in enough light to tell the general it was morning.

Sitting up, he felt all his fifty-six years. The metal shelf with a thin foam mattress played hob with his back. They'd taken his watch, wallet, ID and anything of use, even his shoelaces—as if he'd consider suicide.

By his guess, it was past six in the morning when the slot at the bottom of his door slid open and a breakfast plate appeared.

Breakfast was reconstituted dried eggs—scrambled, of course—and what passed for bacon, probably closer to fowl than porcine. Reconstituted hash browns rounded out the gourmet feast. Knowing he needed whatever nutrients the meal provided, he ate the entire, tasteless pile and then deposited the plate in the door's out-slot.

Several hundred yards from the stockade, newly minted General Bromley fidgeted. On the horns of dilemma, his night had been as bad or worse than Pratt's. The grapevine news about Pratt's attempt to invoke the Twenty-fifth Amendment and remove Wright from office spread like wildfire through the base, with a majority in favor of General Pratt. Bromley knew the court martial would not be fair and, unless something insubordinate occurred, Pratt was as good as dead.

"General, sir, we have to do something." Staff Sergeant Harper echoed his thoughts. "We can't let them execute General Pratt."

"I know, Harper, I know. But what exactly *do* we do? Storm the executive office? Have our own little coup?"

"It would be preferable to leaving that asshole in charge."

Bromley closed his eyes. He felt the beginnings of a tension migraine and it was not even seven a.m. "That is one thing we mustn't do. The chaos would be all the Russians, Chinese and Mexicans would need to swoop in and devour what's left of us."

"But we can't let them execute him."

"We won't. But we have to save Pratt without destroying what little government remains—"

The phone on the general's desk picked that moment to ring, startling them both.

"General Bromley here . . ."

"Sir. We've just received a report from patrols near Rome."

"Good. How soon will that militia mess be cleaned up?"

"Seems they were mostly beat already, sir, due to—let me be sure I have this correct— mushroom poisoning. And get this, it was Lowman's wife that did the poisoning."

Bromley smiled. "If she's a match for Frank Lowman, I can well imagine she did."

"Sir, Sergeant Andrews is requesting permission to arrest and return with Frank Lowman and that Eli guy, but not the whole family."

"Do they say why?"

"Apparently, the Lowmans provided essential combat support against a militia attack at Lowman's daughter's farm."

Knowing he was sticking his neck out, Bromley made a decision. "Bring in Lowman and Eli. Leave the family out of this."

"Yes, sir, I'll pass the word along. Sir . . ."

"Yes?"

"We are with you no matter what."

Damn, did everyone know how conflicted he was? How long before he was in the stockade beside Pratt?

"You have your orders, son. Bromley out." He hung up the phone.

As he sat in the creaking office chair, he had a thought. Maybe, just maybe, Lowman's capture could work to their mutual advantage.

"Harper, don't you have something to do?"

Recognizing a dismissal, Staff Sergeant Harper got to his feet and saluted. "Yes, sir!"

"Good, get moving. I have a lot of thinking to do."

Harper didn't have any idea what was going through General Bromley's head but he knew it involved Lowman and Pratt. This should be interesting.

North of Lake Weiss

The little caravan of Land Rover and dually stopped at Chet Rogers' farm and delivered extra produce from Martha and John's garden. Chet was happy to see Max again.

It was obvious, by how his face lit up when he looked at her, that he was smitten.

"You can come by anytime," he assured them.

"In these times it's good to know reliable, trustworthy folks. We have to all pull together if we're going to survive." Frank shook the young man's hand. "I just wanted to show my gratitude for saving my girl."

"Hey, nothing to it. Glad to." Chet was thoughtful. "There was word on the radio links of a big dustup over in Waleska."

"We ran afoul of the Rome Militia," Max said. "If it weren't for some army guys it could've been real bad."

"Army? What are *they* doing here? Isn't there enough crap in the cities to keep them occupied?" You could tell by his tone he didn't approve of army involvement.

"Well . . ." Max looked over at her dad. He nodded to her. "They were looking for Dad. The president wants him arrested."

"You must've really pissed off that Chinaman, Mr. Lowman." Chet eyed Frank.

"Chinaman?" Frank was puzzled.

"The one that cursed you with interesting times. Life was pretty dull around here until the bunch of you showed up." His eyes twinkled as he teased. "Seriously, what are you gonna do?"

"Well, I have a reprieve until they finish clearing up those militia idiots. I'm going to make the most of it."

"What happens then?"

"Eli and I go into custody. We agreed, to keep them from arresting the whole family."

"The whole family!" Chet was outraged. "That's grossly illegal."

"Welcome to the new world. The Constitution is basically suspended."

"Look, you need me, call on radio channel 14. My call sign is Red Robin."

He pointed at his hair and laughed.

"We don't plan on fighting. We can't lick the entire military. Hopefully there will be reason we can appeal to." Frank couldn't keep defeat out of his expression. "I have to do what is right for the family."

"Well, while you're sorting it out, I'd be glad to help however I can."

"Chet, we might just take you up on that, if you don't mind."

"Heck, this place is so far off the track I'll bet no one but me knows it's here. Those damn hogs destroyed my garden, so other than the food I have put by, there is nothing to defend here. So, like I said, if you need an extra set of hands, give a yell."

Frank could tell Chet was sincere. He also could see the blossoming connection between Max and Chet. It was obvious from how he deferred to her, helping her down from the truck, helping her back up, holding doors . . . It also spoke volumes that the fiercely independent Max allowed it.

"Good to know, Chet. Soon as we find out what's happening, we'll get in touch."

Frank climbed up into the huge dually and fired up the diesel. "Thanks again, Chet."

Katie made sure to hug Chet before climbing into the passenger side. Chet blushed. Max hugged him longer than was necessary and also whispered something in his ear. Whatever she said made him blush more and smile, too. As they drove away, Katie asked her daughter what she'd said that had such an effect.

"I simply told him not to be a stranger and that he was always welcome at my home," Max answered.

"I don't think that'll be a problem, honey." Frank smiled. "However, there may be an issue . . ."

"What?" she asked fearfully.

"Where to get a wedding dress, these days."

"Ow!" Frank flinched as Max hit the side of his head from the backseat. He looked in the mirror to see that her blush nearly matched Chet's.

* * *

The drive to the BOL was uneventful.

George met the small convoy at the gate. "I'm sure glad to see everyone back. Maybe we can get down to just livin'."

Katie and Frank exchanged unhappy glances. If only it were that simple. Over dinner they explained everything to George, including the impending arrest overshadowing the homecoming.

"Well," George said, "we'll deal with it when it happens."

"There is no dealing, George. When Sergeant Andrews or anyone else from the government calls in the marker, Eli and I have to go. It is that or everyone gets arrested and put in that damn camp in Birmingham."

"That's just not right." George crossed his arms.

"Right or wrong doesn't matter. We have to go to save the rest of you."

"Mr. Frank is correct. We have no choice. It will be as Allah wills."

"Allah wills! What a load of horse pucky. It is what President Wright wills, that asshole!"

George stormed away from the table, obviously upset.

"Let him go, Eli." Frank grabbed Eli's shoulder. "'He doesn't mean to offend. He's upset."

"I know, Mr. Frank. I am not offended."

Frank never ceased to be amazed at the calm that seemed to live in Eli.

"OK, let's start planning for the worst. What exactly can we do if—or when—Sergeant Andrews drops the next shoe?"

"Well, that still leaves David, me and George to manage things here," Earl chimed in.

"Earl, dear, what argh Katie an' me? Chop't liver?" Marlene showed the fire of her Irish background.

Earl flinched as if feeling again the hot spaghetti she'd once poured over his head. "You know what I mean, honey."

"Aye, but don't fergit who it was holding off those gits when David was shot!"

She picked up dishes and headed to the outside sink.

"I didn't mean any disrespect. I would never—" Earl stammered.

"It's been stressful the last few days, Earl," Katie said. "She'll get over it, I'm sure. I know what you meant and I'm not offended. I'll talk to her."

She patted Earl's hand before helping Marlene with the dishes and fostering a little woman-to-woman time.

Outside Rome, Georgia

And Lowman BOL

Sergeant Andrews pounded twice on the side of the MRAP. Its loading door shut with a thud of finality on the remaining members of the Peoples Militia of Rome. The cleanup of the group had taken only two days. Most of the remaining members disappeared following the rout of their "brigadier" at Reynolds Farm.

Sergeant Andrews' heart was heavy. He knew his orders; he also knew they were wrong. He had a deep feeling that arresting Frank Lowman and Eli was not right. He knew it was his duty to disobey unlawful orders. However, these weren't normal times. The chain of command was ruptured, perhaps beyond repair. He knew the rumors about President Wright and his son. He also had it on good authority that Lowman had acted with admirable restraint.

"Sergeant, we are ready to load up." Specialist Johnston stood at attention, awaiting orders.

"Alright, load up!" Andrews shook his head sadly as he made up his mind.

"Humvee 1, escort the MRAP back to Birmingham. I will ride with Humvee 2 to pick up Lowman."

As with non-coms since time began, he chose to buck the problem up the chain of command. Deciding moral issues was above his pay grade.

* * *

"And don't forget to wipe!" Max said, looking over her father's shoulder.

Frank carefully dipped the end of the towel in the boiling lid pan and then wiped the rims of each of the glass canning jars. Once the jar lips were clean, he used a magnetic probe to pull a lid from the boiling water and place it on the jar.

"Remember to center it," Max admonished, "or you won't get a good seal."

Placing a finger on the lid, Frank made sure it was centered and the rubber gasket around the edge was making full contact. Then he placed a ring on the jar top and screwed it finger-tight. He used a hot pad to move the finished can of stewed tomatoes over with its brethren, about two dozen, waiting for their turn in the boiling pot for final sterilization and sealing.

Max and Frank were finishing up two days of canning vegetables and other garden produce. Outside in the shade of an oak, Frank had set up two propane-powered burners and a two folding tables. Trailer kitchens didn't have room to can.

Usually, Frank would be in charge of mechanical matters and martial aspects of training, but he was finding the last two days working with Max to be fun and relaxing, although at times she reminded him of his boot camp company commander. Frank removed his ball cap and, taking a handkerchief from his pocket, wiped sweat from his forehead and face.

As he was loading the water bath canner with the next set of cans, the radio at his belt came to life. "Base, this is Rover 1 . . ."

The call was from the observation post at the edge of the Lowman property near County Road 114.

Frank keyed the mic clipped on his shirt. "Rover 1 this is Base. Go ahead."

"Base, we have a military Humvee headed for the driveway. Over."

"Roger that. A Humvee heading for driveway. Base out."

Frank removed the GRILL SERGEANT apron and handed it to Max.

"Oh, Dad, are they going to . . ."

"I don't know, honey. Stay here and watch the canning. Regardless, we'll need food in the next few months."

He hugged her. In the distance he could hear the Humvee engine and the crunch of gravel from the drive.

At the trailer across the clearing from the canning station, Katie was hanging out laundry.

"They're back," was all Frank had to say. She turned and hugged him.

"Maybe they got new orders?" She sounded hopeful.

"We can hope."

The Humvee halted in front of the main trailer and Sergeant Andrews got out.

"Frank, good to see you. Eli here as well?"

"Yes, in the garden," Frank said. "I expect he saw you drive up and will be along shortly."

"Good."

"I don't suppose your orders have changed."

"No, sir. I'm afraid not."

"Any word on General Pratt?"

"He is still under arrest, awaiting court martial."

They all turned as the four-wheeler drove up from the garden. Eli was the sole rider and had his rifle in the scabbard on the side of the ATV.

"Can we take anything with us?"

"Sure. But no weapons. Maybe a change of clothes and toiletry items."

"Care for some tea, Sergeant?" Katie asked, the strain apparent in her voice.

"No, ma'am. But thank you."

"Eli, get a spare set of clothes and whatever else you need," Frank said, turning toward the trailer. "Sergeant, if you'll excuse me, I'll get some extra clothes for myself."

"Yes, sir. Please go ahead."

"It's wrong, you know."

They startled at the voice. It was Max, and she had her AR-15 pointed at the sergeant.

"Max, put that down!" Frank admired her guts, but he knew where this would lead.

"Dad, I'm not going to let him take you."

The driver-side doors flew open and two rifle barrels instantly materialized, aimed directly at Max.

"Max, lower the weapon. We *have* to go."

Frank reached over and grabbed the barrel of Max's AR, forcing it down. "There's been enough killing."

"But you and Eli haven't done anything *wrong*," she pleaded, tears streaming her face.

"Ma'am, we will make sure there is a fair trial," Sergeant Andrews offered.

"With that asshole Wright in charge?" Max looked at him with disgust. "Not very likely."

She dropped the AR to the ground. Katie wrapped her arms around her and they both started crying. Marlene and Earl, out of breath from the run up the drive from the garden, arrived just as Eli returned carrying a small bag.

"I am ready, Mr. Frank."

"Try to keep everyone from killing each other until I get back," Frank said, then went to the main trailer.

"I'll do my best, Frank," Earl said.

"Look, I'm sorry," Sergeant Andrews said. "I'm just following orders."

He looked like he would prefer to be anywhere but here, arresting Frank and Eli.

"Isn't that what that git Lieutenant Calley said about My Lai?"

Marlene's voice was cold, but before things could escalate Frank came out of the main trailer with a small bag.

"OK, let's go. Earl, take care of everyone until I get back."

Frank shook Earl's hand, then hugged and kissed Katie and Max, and hugged Marlene.

Sergeant Andrews wisely stayed silent as they cuffed and loaded Frank and Eli into the Hummer. Everyone stared mutely as the vehicle turned around and headed away down the gravel drive, taking Frank and Eli into a dark future.

***

I hope you enjoyed book two of The World in Darkness series. If you haven't read book one, Prelude to Darkness, I hope you will now! I also have several other titles available if you enjoy my writing style:

Ransom of the Phoenix
Seeds of Wonder
Quest of the Rune Sword
The Mysteries of Rock Lake
Prelude to Darkness
Suppressors: The Shattering
The Emerald Curse

All of my books are available on Amazon, Createspace and for Kindle.

Made in the USA
Monee, IL
15 August 2024

63920755R00125